Escape Your World

Anthology of Award-winning Short Stories

ISBN: 0-9851833-3-0
ISBN-13: 978-0-9851833-3-2

DEDICATION

This anthology is dedicated to those who seek to escape

To the authors featured in this book: Scribes Valley thanks you for your time, patience, trust, and talent.

.

CONTENTS

ESCAPE YOUR WORLD
A Foreword by David L. Repsher, editor

We all have a world that encompasses everything in our lives: family, work, hobbies, bills, worries, playtime, stresses. We have to live our lives, but sometimes we allow ourselves to be overwhelmed by our world. We give in to the pressures of daily living, pushing "me time" to the background, and feel as if our world is "crashing down around our ears." (How many times have you said *that?*)

But there is an escape, and it comes in the form of a book. A book is, physically, a simple thing: a front and back cover with page after page of words and/or pictures in between. You can hold one in your hands and take it wherever you want. Aside from the physical, a book is a transporter—not for your body, but for your mind, your consciousness, and your imagination. Between those simple covers, you can find unlimited worlds to explore, endless places to visit, and countless topics to ponder.

This anthology is one such transporter. Thirteen incredibly talented authors are at the controls, ready to send you into locales, situations, and worlds that you might never have even imagined.

So, sit back, take a deep breath, turn this page, and escape your world!

FIRST PLACE

SUMMER BIRDS ON THE ALBION
©2015 by Kathy Bjornestad

Barton first saw her on the *Albion's* quarterdeck, waif-like, but on the cusp of womanhood, wisps of russet hair escaping from beneath a wide-brimmed bonnet. Her high-waisted gown billowed like a sail in the briny wind. She might have been any English maid returning home from abroad, as displaced among tar buckets and halyards on the East India Company's merchant ship as she had been in the dirty, colorful marketplaces of India's Calcutta.

She shouldn't have been alone, but her companion, a pinch-faced, elderly matron, had fallen victim to seasickness the first night out and had not yet recovered. Though the girl—Lucy, her name was—appeared delicate, in truth, the man decided, she was not. Noting the way she gripped the gunwale, the straight line of her shoulders, the jut of her rather square chin, he supposed she had grown impatient of nursing Mrs. Smith and had slipped away from the closeness of their cabin when sleep took the old woman.

Miss Lucy stood firm against the rolling deck, a packet of letters clenched in her right hand. She grimaced. Her eyebrows knit. Some inner turmoil caused the hand holding the letters to clench, crumpling fragile parchment, but she didn't seem to notice. Her facial muscles twitched and lips mumbled voicelessly in silent argument.

Barton had just decided to join her when another passenger appeared around the mizzenmast. Mr. Charles Everly, the young

9

scientist they had picked up at Sri Lanka, smoothed his rumpled linen shirt (a fruitless effort, for his cravat remained askew), and slicked back windblown hair, which immediately blew up again in a brown tangle. His normally distracted-looking gray eyes appeared at this moment sharp as sunlight reflected off metal. They pierced Miss Lucy like twin stars.

She was by no means a beautiful girl, though her position as the only female under thirty aboard the *Albion* had made the male crew and passengers tolerant of this defect. Barton had noticed several sailors casting wistful looks her way, but she paid no heed. When Mr. Everly's quiet footfalls carried him near, she turned, and a curtain descended on her inner dialogue. From his deck chair, Barton heard her exclaim, "Mr. Everly!" and a saw a blush rise to her cheeks.

The young man nodded, a quiet smile transforming his tanned, ordinary face into something more vibrant. Mr. Everly pointed to a gull suspended on the stiff breeze, a broad-chested fellow with sharp, avaricious eyes and a curved beak. Barton couldn't make out what conversation followed, but from Mr. Everly's gestures, it appeared he was enlightening Lucy on the mysteries of the avian species.

As a retiring missionary, Barton considered himself a fair judge of man's nature. His work had been with the soul, but understanding the intricacies of the human mind had made him successful in converting many heathens. Now he was returning to Shropshire, England, so that he might expire in the land of his birth. What else to do besides die after a life spent in far off places filled with dark magic and tropical climes, mystical shamans and sloe-eyed women? He had thought nothing more in this life could surprise him, yet he now found himself surprised, and, yes, *intrigued.*

The couple retreated from the railing and sat down just past a pile of hemp rope. Pretending to read his dog-eared Bible, Barton caught snatches of their conversation.

"I have another book you might enjoy, Miss Lucy," Charles Everly was saying in a mild, hesitant tone.

"Oh, Mr. Everly?"

"Have you heard of Maria Merian?" A pause. "She was a woman

scientist who studied entomology. Her work, unfortunately, is not well-read, but brilliant in its method. In a time when creatures with the ability to metamorphose were considered evil, she proved that such shape-changers were simply a fascinating part of nature."

"Do you mean butterflies, for instance?"

Mr. Everly nodded energetically. "Exactly. Summer birds, she called them. Isn't that poetic?"

"Summer birds," Miss Lucy repeated.

Barton slid a glance toward the young people and startled. When he had first seen the girl, he thought her caterpillar-plain. But now, Mr. Everly's enthusiasm touched her like sunlight, transforming a stoic countenance into a lively flame. Towards the start of their journey, he had thought, *this girl is similar to me, a creature on the fringes of life.* But now he realized he was wrong. Like an insect tearing free of its cocoon, she glowed with life.

Barton worried his lower lip. Everly had placed a brown hand familiarly over Lucy's pale one. Mrs. Smith would not approve.

Oblivious to Barton's attention, the companions rose. Mr. Everly took Miss Lucy's arm, and they strolled off. The packet of letters lay forgotten on the deck chair. A breeze made the pages flutter like a pigeon's tail feathers, and, afraid the missives might decide to fly, he rose stiffly and scooped them up. He started after their owner, then realized she was already too far away for his arthritic legs to intercept. Barton had no mind to call out, so he tucked the letters into his coat and retired to his cabin, where the packet lay atop a sea chest, untouched, while he went to dinner.

Neither Miss Lucy nor Charles Everly appeared that night, an event too coincidental to be benign occurrence, yet the grizzled captain, along with a middle-aged couple returning to England for the birth of their first grandchild, seemed unsuspicious. Mrs. Leigh-Carlton lost no opportunity in opening the conversation with, "I see poor Miss Lucy isn't with us tonight. Is she feeling unwell?"

The captain, a red-cheeked, jowly man with tropic-blue eyes, sipped his ale, then replied, "I believe she is once again nursing the unfortunate Mrs. Smith, whom, it appears, is never to achieve her sea legs."

Mrs. Leigh-Carlton tutted, "Such a shame."

Her husband tried to intercept the conversation with, "I recall your first trip overseas, my dear, and the horrible..."

But his wife was not to be distracted, and with an impatient glance his way, she continued, "Such a plain little thing, Miss Lucy, and yet so polite, so unassuming. Could no other husband be discovered for her in India?"

The captain cleared his throat, clearly uncomfortable, and shrugged.

Mr. Leigh-Carlton seized the opportunity to interject and declared, "It was, of course, a small community of foreigners. And at five and twenty, Miss Lucy is no dewy maiden. Had she more fortune, she might have found another man to marry her, but as it is..."

Mrs. Leigh-Carlton joined him in sympathetic head-shaking.

Barton stayed silent, observing but not partaking, as was his wont. He took in the Leigh-Carltons, middle-class social climbers who possessed the manners of the bourgeoisie, but also a subtle, greedy crassness covered only by a thin veneer of Christian charity. He did not care for them.

Mrs. Leigh-Carlton clicked her tongue again. "But what will Miss Lucy do in England? Will relatives take her in?"

"I believe there is an older sister," the captain replied. "With a parcel of children."

"Ah, I see." A look of pity flitted over Mrs. Leigh-Carlton's face, and Barton wondered if he had misjudged her. But then she shrugged. "At least the poor girl shall be cared for. It is not a life *I* would have chosen, but to each her own." She slid a smug glance toward her browbeaten husband, who studied his last bite of salt pork with dubious attention.

Barton almost spoke in defense of Miss Lucy, whom he very much doubted had *chosen* to nursemaid her sister's children. If she *had* agreed to it, her aim had likely been to unburden her parent.

No one mentioned Mr. Charles Everly. He often forgot to attend dinner in favor of writing in his scientific journal. What conversation he possessed did not seem to suit the Leigh-Carltons or the captain, for neither shared his passion for academic pursuits. Barton had spoken to Mr. Everly a time or two, however, and found him to be an engaging fellow if one knew how to listen—a man of books, not of the world. Yet the world seemed to fascinate him much as it did Barton, as something to be observed for its small miracles and surprising patterns. *How lucky I have been,* thought he, *to have seen so much of it. But now all that is over.*

Shaking off a sudden melancholia, Barton excused himself and retreated to his cabin. Just before he reached it, a slight form materialized out of the dimness below decks. Miss Lucy. He stopped her as she edged around him in the narrow passageway and said, "Pardon me, Miss, but you left your letters in a deck chair, and I have them in my cabin. I can fetch them for you."

Her eyebrows rose like wings, and color stained her cheeks. She seemed distracted, and it took a moment for her green eyes to focus on him. "Oh," she said, twisting her hands together. "You needn't have bothered, really. I'm finished with them. In fact…" a violent trembling took hold of her voice, "throw them overboard, please. Or do anything with them. I care not. I shan't want them back."

He hadn't thought he could be shocked anymore, but this reply held him speechless. Letters were a precious commodity to be treasured and reread. He stuttered, "As you wish, Miss," then started to add more, but she had already curtsied and turned away.

The packet, tied with blue ribbon, had slipped from the chest onto the floor. He picked it up, lit a kerosene lamp, and sat down stiffly on his narrow bunk. Barton stared at the bundle. *Throw them overboard.* He repeated her words to himself. Yet he was curious. Why did the letters mean so little to her? He chided himself for being just such a busybody as Mrs. Leigh-Carlton, yet his thick-knuckled fingers fumbled with the ribbon, and it fell away.

> *Dearest Lucy,*
>
> *I have just received your latest letter, and I must scold you for being neglectful. Does Calcutta society keep you so busy that you cannot take time for your poor sister, tucked into the boring*

countryside whilst you dance and socialize your way through a foreign and exotic locale? But do not pity me, dear sister, for tomorrow we dine at the Ashcrofts. Anna will attend, as will John Butler. You recall how we played together as children? He is much changed since the war, and walks with a heavy limp. I thought at one time he might do for you, but as he is now engaged to Clara Jones, I must rely on Father to find you a suitable husband....

Barton stopped reading and frowned. The lamp's flame danced wickedly behind its smoke-blackened pane. He tossed the first letter on the coverlet and picked up a second.

Oh Dear Lucy,

I just received word from father of your engagement! Please forgive any attempts at matchmaking in my last letter, although I must say that this Harry Gerard seems a bit old. Is he really so rich as to make his antiquity bearable? Do you like him? Or is this marriage solely Father's doing? A bright smile will compensate for a plain visage, I always said to you, but that is beside the point now, I suppose. A husband is a husband, and men are all very much alike, are they not? I barely see John, what with the Lords meeting in London, and the constant flurry of activity with the children. I so wish there was someone here to help me....

This letter joined its sister. A third, dated some time later, began,

Dearest Lucy,

How sorry I was to hear that your promised husband succumbed to a fever and is no more. Horrid India! How relieved I will be to see you removed from that place. On a brighter note, I wish you very happy on your twenty-fifth birthday. As you recall, little Geoffrey's birthday is also this month. How time flies! Already he runs about and will soon be in breeches. Thank heavens, as baby Adelaide consumes much of my time. How good it will be to have you here. Poor Nurse Beckett is quite beside herself managing the older three, and as for Catherine and James, I fear they are running roughshod over our governess, a Miss Wortham, recently employed. Poor thing. She was brought up a gentlewoman, but alas, like so many governesses, has come down in station and had to find employment. Is it not fortunate that you, dear sister, have family to take you in?

Yes indeed, Barton thought bitterly. *How fortunate.*

His sleep that night was troubled. He dreamed he was a gull. The sea sang to him, each note a shimmer of purple and gray. He pushed toward the sun, closer and closer, its warmth like a woolen blanket upon his back. Then the breeze died, and he plummeted down to white-toothed waves. The wind current caught him just in time. A fish jumped, and he snapped it up. He waltzed among the clouds until a ship sailed into view, and insatiable hunger drove him toward salt-rimed decks and bread crusts from weathered sailors.

His point of view changed, and suddenly he *was* a sailor. He smiled at a pair of gulls. They knew him and cawed fiercely. Though he could no longer understand their language, they spoke to some secret knowledge within him, whispering, *freedom, freedom*. The birds wheeled and drifted toward far-off cliffs painted a watercolor pink. Tossed like bits of paper, the gulls shrank until distance and forgetfulness consumed them.

Barton woke to the sound of loud voices overhead. Filaments of light pierced his tiny porthole, through which the minarets and mosques of Cádiz, Spain, were barely visible. The *Albion* bobbed at anchor.

He dressed and went above, where the first mate was just lowering a longboat into balmy waters. Two pastel parasols bloomed on a green sea and shrouded the boat's occupants, but he guessed Mrs. Leigh-Carlton and Miss Lucy must be among them. As it turned out, Mr. Charles Everly and Mr. Leigh-Carlton were also aboard, along with two sailors. The captain joined the man at the railing, saying, "If you want, we can pull 'er back up. Mr. Everly disembarks here, and the others decided to join him for a day ashore."

Glancing again toward the small boat, which now almost brushed the waves, Barton noticed a trunk occupying one end. Faint dismay took hold of him. He had not realized Mr. Everly would not be accompanying them all the way to England. "Nay," he told the captain, "It would be too tiring an outing for these old bones."

The captain slapped him on the back. "We are only as old as we feel, Mr. Barton."

Barton formed a smile but remained silent, watching as the boat was released and bucked along gentle waves, propelled by the two oar-wielding sailors. Other ships basked in the Andalucían haze, and far off, a dock bustled with ant-sized workers. But Barton had eyes only for the shore-bound boat. Something niggled at him—a sort of longing, or perhaps a memory. Feelings of loss tangled with a strange euphoria. He rubbed his temples, thinking he had better sit.

The first mate brought him water and drew a deck chair into the shade of the fore sail, asking if he felt unwell. He shook his head.

Barton lounged there even after the shadows withdrew and the harsh sun beat down on his head. He observed while another longboat drew up to shore, and later returned with supplies and cargo bound for England. A deckhand mending sail nearby cast him occasional glances. Perhaps the man worried he might die of the heat, and the crew would be obliged to dispose of his remains.

Yet he felt oddly well. As morning stretched into afternoon, and the sun rose plump and joyful in a plate glass sky, those pulsing rays infused him with new energy. Life was not seeping out of him, as appearances might suggest; instead, it seeped *into* him. His mysterious and conflicted emotions battled, and gradually a boisterous feeling— the kind a youth experiences upon a virgin trip out into the world— overcame regret and sadness. He did not try to explain it, only soaked it in.

Not until sunset spilled across the horizon did the last boat return. Barton squinted, shaded his eyes, then absorbed what his subconsciousness had known long before. He thought of the seagulls from his dream. He thought of Miss Lucy and her letters, of Mr. Everly and his book about the female scientist and the summer birds. One pastel parasol appeared over the railing's edge. Mrs. Leigh-

Cartlon's frizzy head emerged from under the lacy fringe. Barton waited. He envisioned a monarch butterfly landing briefly on the brim, mistaking it perhaps for a giant flower, then fluttering away into the dying light, a speck of color—smaller, smaller, gone.

Miss Lucy had flown.

There would be scandal, a fruitless search (he hoped), and finally, embarrassed forgetfulness. Miss Lucy's sister would sigh self-righteously when she chanced to remember her sister, but Barton, from his small cottage in Shropshire, would smile as he gazed beneath the ruffled waves of the pond where he fished, and dreamed, and hoped.

About the author:

Kathy Bjornestad is a public school librarian from Wyoming who loves reading and writing. She has been a novel finalist in both the Colorado Gold Writing Contest and the Pikes Peak Writing Contest. In 2011 her novel, *Legend*, won a Wyoming Creative Writing Fellowship. She has published essays in *Christian Science Monitor* and recently received an honorable mention for the Neltje Blanchan Award. Her first love is young adult science fiction, but she enjoys writing in all forms.

SECOND PLACE

PROMETHEUS
©2015 by Joseph Horst

Sizzle.

Most people only hear the roar of a fire, the comforting warmth and security. They don't hear the whispers underneath and inside that roar, nothing like the three smiling elves on a cereal box.

Snap. Some things—including flesh—don't just break apart clean as they burn; sometimes they slowly bend and curl until finally submitting.

Crackle. Gasoline and tree sap both hiss as they burn, like a sustained whisper of danger.

Pop. Pine cones pop when they burn. So do chestnuts. But those are nice, safe images…propane tanks pop too. So does bone.

Sweat.

It's dark. And tight. And he hates it, but he crawls through it. He recites the alphabet—backwards—to keep the gnawing claustrophobia away. *It's only 20 yards, it's only 20 yards…*and it's another step closer. He crawls out the end of the rectangular metal tube and walks back to the starting point. Still not fast enough. Do it again.

Smoke.

The frigid night air misted around the small body as he carried it away from the smoking house. He walked around the far side of the engine to escape the teary gaze of the child who stood wrapped in a blanket with a red cross on it. Let the morning news make a bad night even worse. Let the boy hope.

He gently laid the bundle of fur on another blanket and stared down at it. Stuff like this shouldn't happen.

This was his job…his duty.

He was supposed to save them.

* * *

He wakes from a fitful sleep, the sheets crumpled around his sweat-slick body. What roused him? Was it a half-heard shout in response to his dreams? Or was it the overwhelming need that even now starts gnawing at his insides? It doesn't matter. He's up now.

Washing the black soot that seems to find its way on every place of his body, he tries to recall last night. Leaning on the shower wall, the images flash like heat lightning. Too much to bear, he sticks his head under the freezing water to relieve the pain. Climbing out of the shower, he catches a glimpse of himself in the mirror. He turns away, vaguely wondering what happened to the youth he remembered.

He walks to the window, weaving his way through the nests of papers that encircle candles like halos. The window opens with a tortured squeal, but the tremendous heat in the room stays. Leaning his head against the sill, the murmurings of the city greet him. The air is still and hot, teasing his senses with the promise of another Santa Ana day. He squints to see the rising sun, but the city sky-line blocks his pathetic worship.

He turns, half expecting the room to be different than when he walked through it last. His bleary vision takes in the mound of discarded matchbooks on the table with disinterest.

That's not what he needs.

Neither are the nests of homage scattered about the floor like anthills in the desert.

He spots the half-full cigarette pack lying on the floor next to the refrigerator, with the matchbook cover that proclaims the wonders of some dirty country bar gleaming at him through the condom-like cellophane wrapper. He reaches down, picks up the pack, and withdraws a crumpled cigarette. He strikes a match and draws the death-smoke deep into himself, feeling the tension of the night expelled with the smoke that gathers in a cloud around his head. Before he can wave the match out, his eyes alight on the flickering flame. He hears that tiny, leering voice once again and loses himself.

* * *

He dreams...

Of armor-clad men charging over island lands, glass breaking at their feet and sweet-smelling liquid covering them. Of those men screaming as flames fall from the sky and set the liquid afire. Of other men smothering their comrades, oftentimes with their own bodies, to save them from this new weapon.

Of an eight-pointed cross, either Maltese or Florian, each point with its own value and meaning. Pride. Loyalty. Honor. Charity. Gallantry. Generosity. Dexterity. And possibly the most important and overreaching value of all: protection of the weak.

Of the ladder, the pick axe, and the pike pole. Tools handed down from the Crusades. Of the bugle and helmet, leadership and safety surrounding a scramble borne from generations before.

He wakes...

By a wordless shout he's not sure who has caused it though he sleeps alone...

With tears hot in his eyes, cool on his cheeks...are they pride? Sorrow? Joy?

With the weight of the graying remnants of his dream crushing him until it forces an explosive inhale of air back into his body. He can still see the scramble above his head, like the after-image of a forked lightning bolt. It slowly fades away until his eyes close again.

* * *

This was literally shit work, but he didn't care.

Anybody else would have groaned to hear the tones and whistles at two-thirty in the morning on a humid summer evening. But this was his first call...*ever*...and all the dispatcher had said was "car versus horse".

His mom pulled the car over on the northbound side of the

highway and he jumped out of it before it had even really stopped, before she could yell at him to be careful crossing the road. He quickstepped it across half of the four-lane highway, shrugging his jacket on and hiking his turnout pants a little higher around his fourteen-year-old waist.

As he walked through the short grass of the median, he marveled at the damage to the two-door red Nissan. The front axle of the car had broken under some immense weight, pushing both front wheels even further apart. Half of the windshield was completely missing and the roof of the car had been cut off, probably to get to the driver. *Did anybody really survive that?*

Not the horse. No way could it have survived judging by the brains, guts, undigested food and shit—mounds of it stinking up the night—strewn on the highway. He picked his way through the remnants and strained to see past the strobing white and red lights. He could barely make out a large, darker lump on the right side of the road that must have been the rest of the animal.

"Whereyatakkinme?" Somehow, some way, the driver—pretty drunk by the way he had just slurred four words into one long one—had survived the crash and was being loaded into the ambulance parked in the right lane of the southbound highway.

Before he could get over to the EMT guys and ask them what was going on, the lieutenant had walked up. "Grab a hose and clean this mess up."

"Yes, sir!" The lieutenant ignored him and walked away. He ran over to the tanker and grabbed the nozzle of the reel hose. Another volunteer firefighter helped him wrestle the water-filled hose—he was strong enough to do it himself, but he'd get in trouble if he tried—and he opened the nozzle to start the clean-up.

He heard a loud scrape of metal on asphalt and watched a beat-up yellow bulldozer—*a bulldozer!*—lumber to the side of the highway. Metal scraped again against the road, then a wet sucking sound of the horse being loaded into the scoop.

He watched the powerful stream of water mix the horse's bodily fluids into one dark-brown color and push it onto the grass on the side of the road. *Oh man, oh man, oh man.* The odor of the shit, brains and guts made his stomach churn and nose burn, but there was absolutely nothing that could wipe the ultra-wide grin off of his face.

I fucking love this.

* * *

Fire and ice.

The flame leaps from non-existence, searching for sustenance. It catches the paper's edge, starts slow, then consumes with a vengeance. White turns to brown turns to black. Its hypnotic spell weaves pathways through his mind, gobbling oxygen and his thoughts.

What beast lies there? What manner of consciousness resides within that small yellow and blue abode? Given the chance, it will grow—it will conquer. Until it dominates all, only then will it perform the ultimate martyrdom: consuming itself.

Another match struck.

Another paper torn.

His habit begins again.

* * *

The match had gone out a long time ago and burned his first two fingers. He barely feels the pain, for his fingers have blisters upon blisters. One more sign of his faith will make no difference. He drops the charred matchstick in the sink, making a vague mental note to throw away the pile of used matches already present. He pulls on yesterday's clothes, absentmindedly wiping at the black patches on his knees and elbows. He brushes his dirty hair back and opens the door. Even though the doorway is still shrouded in shadows, he puts on his black Ray-Ban sunglasses. If he didn't, he'd probably forget and be lost in the first opening the sun shone through, staring at it until his sight burned. The day awaits.

He walks down the street, aimlessly watching the bums and passersby. Then the siren call of his nemesis breaks through his reverie. He turns to look as the wail grows in pitch and volume, soon forcing him to throw his hands over his ears in a desperate attempt to block the intruder. His foe speeds by in the all-too-familiar elongated truck, painted in the obscene parody of his only true love. He mouths words of passion and fury, but his voice is still too hoarse for the disciples of his enemy to hear him. This is good, he finally realizes, for undue attention would hamper him in his final work.

With an effort, he turns from the persistent shrieking and continues his walk. But the swinging stoplight in the wind catches his eye and draws him, with a faint sigh of protest, relentlessly to the past that he abhors.

* * *

Red.

He sees himself as a boy, crouching in the bushes around his house. He watches with rapt attention as the mixture of Styrofoam, newspaper and leaves catch with the ocean breeze into a small but entrancing fire. He does not realize at the time that he is having his first erection.

Green.

He looks down at the slip of paper that has turned his life upside down. Their insincere regret at not allowing him to join their elite fighting corps burns deep within his chest. Then he realizes the ultimate revenge. If you can't beat the enemy, join him.

Yellow.

He is watching his first work. It was messy and he almost got caught, but it all worked out in the end. He thrusts his hands deeper into his pockets, hiding the fresh soot marks and burns. He stands at the fringe of the crowd, finally realizing his true purpose in life.

Red once again.

The cycle repeats.

* * *

She just didn't get it.

He wedged his three-year-old body between the window and the couch, his face squished against the glass, his eyes wide and searching. Even at this age, he could tell the difference between a police car and a fire truck by sound alone. Hear the police sirens wail; he couldn't care less…but he would have run out to chase that unique warble of a fire engine's siren if they had let him.

For a brief instant, the elongated red engine slid past the window and he howled. Though it was only for a second, every detail was etched in his mind. From the hoses, to the ladders, to the gleaming metal. As the engine's siren faded away, he ran through the house trying to mimic it with his own young voice. His mother would have tried to make him stop, like she had so many times before, if it wasn't for the wide smile and joy plastered on his face.

She just didn't get it.

Those tones and whistles...his fiancée calls them "annoying" and "terrible." He thinks they are quite possibly the best music he has ever heard. He checks his bunker gear almost on the hour; it doesn't matter that he hasn't moved the red duffle bag since the last time.

Nomex hood carefully folded and laid inside his helmet.

Jacket with reflective stripes that glow all on their own hung on a solitary hook.

Gloves resting on a coil of rope.

His turnout pants arranged around his boots in a careful pile...just jump in, pull up and go where that wonderful music tells him his destiny lies.

He shifts the bag half an inch and steps back to his bed. The logo—that cross with the scramble in the middle that he's memorized and can see even during the black of night—has to be— *has to be*—where he can see it almost without turning his head.

His fiancée had moved it once and he had pitched a fit. "Don't touch my gear!," he screamed. He solemnly put the duffle bag back in its place. He sat on the edge of his bed and just stared at it, the fact that she was standing in his doorway forgotten. She looked at him for one, now two beats, shook her head and walked out of the room.

* * *

He cracks his neck twice—once to the right, once to the left—and sighs. They'd already been there four hours, and they still had a number of interviews to go. He looks over the table at the various men sitting with him: a captain, another lieutenant like himself, two firefighters from the house, and another man from a different district whose rank he can't remember.

When the next applicant walks in, the lieutenant automatically gives the low sign to the other board members. They had worked out a system before this all started; who wants to be the "bad guy"?

Every board has a member who would intentionally push the applicant, see how much he can take under pressure. The low sign was their way of saying "I'm up" and that he would play the heavy for this particular guy.

He can't tell you why he doesn't like this guy, though…there's just something *off* about him. Maybe it's the way the guy's suit just seems dusty or the way he constantly brushes at his elbows like he's cleaning them off. Or maybe it's the way his black Ray-Bans are *still* on his face, even inside. He watches the guy finally take off the Ray-Bans as he sits down in front of the board, and it's another nail in the coffin. Shifty, squinty eyes.

"Why do you want to work in this industry?" The lieutenant can see out of the corner of his eye that the other members are taken aback a little, shooting him looks that they try to hide from the guy. Usually, they start off with some softballs, a preamble of sorts that lets the applicant at least feel a little more comfortable. Not this time, though …

"Uh, well…I like firefighting." The guy's eyes squint more as he tries to look at each board member.

"You *like* firefighting?" The lieutenant looks at the other men at the table and can tell just by the looks on their faces that they agree this guy isn't prepared in the least. "You mean, like you like chocolate or baseball?"

The guy's eyes focus on the lieutenant alone as another board member—probably one of the firefighters—can't hold back a chuckle. "No…nothing like that," the guy replies coldly. "I actually love it; it's my calling."

Not in my house, it isn't. "So, why should we hire you?"

It's almost like there isn't anybody else in the room but the lieutenant and this guy as the guy leans forward and stares at him. "Why *shouldn't* you hire me?" the guy retorts. "You're not going to find anyone better equipped than me."

"Really?" This guy's attitude was just making things worse. "OK, if you're so well-equipped, then what's your greatest weakness?"

"I don't allow any weaknesses." The long silence that follows this wild statement finally breaks through to the guy a little. He shifts in his seat and looks down at his lap. Without looking up, the guy continues.

"Ummm…I mean…if I had to come up with something, I guess I'd have to say it's my passion." He looks up at the board, but doesn't find any help there. "I was *meant* for this."

The lieutenant looks down at his evaluation sheet and pretends to take notes, when in fact all that he's writing is the word *No* over and over again on top of itself. Even though he doesn't want to, he figures he'll give the guy one last shot to save himself.

"OK, you're meant for this? Tell me what motivates you…*why* are you meant for this?"

For maybe the first time, the guy looks interested and invested. "Fire motivates me. Fire fascinates me. We must understand it, respect it. We must study it…*explore* it. What other job do we have than to take it apart piece by piece until we serve each other equally?"

We? No one is chuckling now…in fact, no one is looking at the guy either. All of the board members either shuffle papers or fake taking notes as the silence draws on. The guy looks at each member until he's back staring at the lieutenant, who finally breaks the silence.

"OK…thanks for coming in. We'll be in touch."

The guy stays seated for a long moment until he puts on his Ray-Bans with a swift, jerky movement. He stands and stomps out of the room with his head down.

* * *

"Fire…Flame…Love."

He falls back into the present with an almost audible thump. He realizes that the various pedestrians have been looking at him with wary eyes and muttered grumblings. Embarrassed to be praising his secret master in public, he lowers his head to avoid confrontation and stumbles into a trot.

They'll see.

They'll all see.

It won't be long.

He returns home, looking over his shoulder and going around blocks twice to ensure that no one is following him. He closes the door behind himself quickly so that his prying neighbors can get no glimpse of the interior. *Has there been someone here?* Things seem just a little out of order, like someone picked them up and tried to put them back in the same exact place. But his blueprints are safe underneath the loose floorboard in his bedroom and the hair he placed over it was still in place. If there was someone here before, all they saw was a dilapidated room that looked like street bums had slept in it. Nothing suspicious here.

He walks into the bathroom and turns the tap on. With a groan, water flows through the rusted pipes and into the basin. After the water changes from a dull brown to a light gray—the clearest it's going to get—he cups his hands under the stream and splashes ice-cold water onto his face. Repeating this act twice more, he looks into the cracked mirror over the porcelain sink. *Who is this guy?* He leans forward until his head touches the glass, searching the eyes for some glint of revelation. Light seems to dance within their depths, mocking his attempts to discover their secrets. The rest of the mirror turns a dark gray, leaving only two red pinpoints where his eyes are. Again, as with the stoplight, he is led down the tunnel of remembrance.

* * *

Blood and tears.

His vision triples as his work is strewn out before him. He doesn't know if they're tears of sadness or heat; he doesn't care. Only the work matters. The beast lunges at him, but years of experience and pain have taught him quick reflexes. He backs further into the doorway, surveying the interior with a look not unlike the one a proud father gives a loved son. The flames start to lick at the base of the walls, turning the dark wood to an even darker shade of death. His masterpiece has yet to be fulfilled, but this token should appease the hunger of the beast.

He falls to his knees in reverence and awe of his master's power. Only through this work can he be saved; only through the fire can he live. He holds his head in his hands and weeps in gratitude; the tears sizzle on the boards at his feet. He hates to get up and leave, but more work beckons. He casts a final glance over his shoulder, the ever-increasing flames flickering in his Ray-Bans like a vast mirror.

* * *

He finds himself lying in bed with his arm thrown over his eyes in a pathetic attempt to protect himself from the visions. They're coming more and more often. What used to be a seldom occurrence has grown into a daily torture that he fears may lead to his defeat before having completed his masterpiece. Though he had been waiting for a sign that he should begin his final devastation and ultimate revenge, he must start soon before he loses his sanity.

Maybe these visions are the sign he's been looking for. But that would mean that his master had been torturing his faithful servant even after all of his offerings. He pushes aside that unclean thought before it can lead to others. Only through his work can he possibly redeem himself from the earthly mire that he is stuck in. Any thought contrary to that only leads to doubt, disbelief, and damnation.

He gets out of bed and kneels down next to the loose floorboard. Carefully laying the strand of hair to the side, he pries up the board and withdraws the blueprints. As he stands and unrolls them onto the bed, a small smile creeps onto his face. Here is all the information he will need to bring down his nemesis, everything waiting for him to provide that final spark to achieve immortality.

He is in the lair of his enemy.

He is indestructible.

He cannot fail.

* * *

He shines the new badge until he swears it glows.

A shield actually, not to protect him from harm but to commemorate his brothers who have given their lives, the life he would just as willingly give. A shield made up of four scrolled triangles to form the historical cross. Though he values the new word on the top of the cross—Captain—he still has the first badge ever pinned to his chest.

Every badge, from his first to this one, holds the scramble of firefighter's tools in the center to show ever-readiness, surrounded by an unbroken gold circle to show dedication and commitment. The deep red throughout the badge intertwines his duty, fear, passion, and fury.

As his mind races and tires before sleep can claim him, he sometimes thinks he hears voices in the wind. Voices that he's almost convinced himself say the words he learned so long ago: Pride. Loyalty. Honor. Charity. As he drifts off before the voices can finish their litany, he shies away from one thought...maybe the voices whisper something else.

* * *

Light and dark.

At times when he is deep in his work, he hears voices speaking his name. Soft and sibilant, they hiss and thrum in exultation of his devotion. He may doubt himself in the dark of night when he's lying sweating in his bed, but when the flame leaps up to conjure its brothers, he knows that he is righteous. All the doubts fade away; all the earthly concerns disappear in that faint *scrratchhh* of the sulfur tip hitting the brown striking bar.

Fire: a long drawn-out sigh of ecstasy.

Flame: a spurt of joy that rushes to occupy everything.

Love: a feeling of awe at the power that he has been given.

* * *

He crouches in the dark basement, waiting for the last sounds of his enemies moving within the building to cease. It was risky sneaking into this of all places, but he knew now was the time. Though the building is never entirely empty, his work should be furious enough to prevent any attempts at rescue. How fitting for this building, devoted as it is to stopping his master's work, to succumb to the relentless power of the flame.

This would be his masterpiece.

Now all would give his master the respect that was due.

He moves stealthily, making no noise except for the occasional rustle of the newspapers as he puts them in their strategic places. He has generally stuck to simple gasoline fire, but this is his masterpiece; it *must* be unique.

He looks around the smelly basement one last time before he starts the ultimate expression of his adoration. The papers hold symmetry about them, spread out in a pentagon that covers the entire floor. Starting from a large pile of kerosene-soaked newspapers in the center of the pentagon, he leaves trails of rags leading to mid-sized piles at the various geometrical points. He knows from the blueprints that the floors, ceilings, and roof have been constructed with three by ten inch wood joists. That ensures that his masterpiece will reach optimum heat in the shortest time. Nothing will prevent it.

He walks into the center of the pentagon, facing the largest pile of newspapers.

He kneels in front of it, his hands pressed together in prayer with the matchbook between them.

He tears out the lone match, symbolizing his quest for atonement.

He lights the match and places it against the edge of the newspapers. The fire starts slowly, then speeds up as it catches the faint whiffs of kerosene. He stays there for a moment, savoring the sight that will soon grow into the biggest feat of his career.

He hears the voices again, small and quiet at first like a breeze against his brow. As he falls to one knee, their chants become a small roar between his temples, drowning out all but the most primal thoughts.

He has no idea how long he kneels there, but when he stands and turns around to escape before the alarm can sound, he sees his error.

He has stayed too long in his adoration.

Though the pentagon seemed a fitting symbol to begin his work with, it is now his downfall. The rag trails have died down to embers, but that's not what stops him. The five main points of the pentagon are mini-furnaces, belching black, acrid smoke that makes his eyes water and his lungs burn. He has no idea where the fire door is now; all he sees is the rolling blackness edging closer to him.

He has nowhere to turn but back to the center fire. He is trapped by that which he has created.

He turns, seeing the fire for what it really is for the first and last time of his life. He had no control over the beast; any such presumption has vanished with the intense heat. As he falls to his knees, he realizes that self-sacrifice is the only true gift he can give. The flames again whisper his name over and over; in one last effort, he outstretches his arms and falls into their fiery embrace.

* * *

The captain walks through the drenched remains of the firehouse's basement. *Lucky that someone smelled kerosene and came down to investigate.* If they hadn't, the old building would have gone up like a torch. Not that it mattered to the bastard who had tried to torch the place.

The guy had been overcome by smoke inhalation and burned beyond any hope of identification, except maybe by dental records. The captain had stopped the EMTs as they rolled his body out and forced them to open the body bag. He spat on the man's charred and cracked Ray-Bans, now melted into his face. *Serves him right for trying to set fire to a fire station of all places.*

The captain caresses one of the now-blackened beams that support the old building. Tightening his grip until the tops of his fingers are embedded in the sodden wood, the captain mentally repeats the vow he has always made ever since he became a firefighter.

I will do all in the power given to me to prevent this from happening again.

I am indestructible.

I cannot fail.

About the author:

Joseph Horst received his Master's degree in English, with a concentration in Creative Writing, in 2005 from East Carolina University. His full-length stage play "Enemies", won 7th place in the 76th Annual Writer's Digest Writing Competition (Stageplay) in 2007 and received an Honorable Mention in the 2011 Ohio State University at Newark's Inaugural Play Competition. In 2012, Horst's ten-minute play "Calliope" was performed in the "8x10" Ten Minute Play Festival in Napa, CA. In 2013, his short story "Old Glory" was published in the inaugural issue of the Slippery Elm literary journal.

THIRD PLACE

THE LAST ORDEAL OF JAMES WILLOUGHBY
©2015 by Jeff Spitzer

Opinions differed about James Willoughby. To some he was a brilliant naturalist, a meticulous observer of plants and animals in the Great Smoky Mountains. He discovered more species of salamanders than all his contemporaries combined. He published studies on the hibernation behavior of bats, the life cycles of aquatic insects, and the recovery of ramp (a.k.a. wild leek) populations. His works were required reading in advanced biology courses.

But to those who had actually met him, Willoughby was a hopeless fruitcake. He showed up at conferences in tattered denim and mud-caked hiking boots. He was often heard talking to himself, even debating himself. Though physically attractive and robust, he was socially awkward, sometimes ducking behind doors to avoid his colleagues. He had no friends or family and spent most of his time in the woods, as far from humanity as he could get.

Probably because of his odd behavior, doubts about his scientific credibility arose in certain quarters. Attempts to reproduce his work yielded inconclusive results. There was talk of a committee to investigate his research. Then one day, as if to escape his detractors, he set out on a mountain trail and never returned.

Willoughby remained in oblivion for over a decade. His name suddenly resurfaced when some hikers discovered an uninhabited cave in a remote area of the Smokies and found a stack of mildewed notebooks marked J.W. The hikers spent two days reading. Then, astonished and confused, they emptied their backpacks, crammed in the notebooks, scrambled down the mountain, and headed to the nearest police station. Soon the old controversies about James Willoughby were reignited.

The fate of Willoughby himself remains unknown, although many who have studied his strange legacy have formed their own opinions. A condensation of the events he recorded is presented here.

FROM THE JOURNALS OF JAMES WILLOUGHBY
May 22—Cataloguing saprophytes at the higher elevations

This morning I had the most astounding encounter of my life. It occurred on the periphery of a heath bald (elev. approx. 5000 ft.). I had awakened just before dawn and emerged from my tent into a silken mist. Falling away behind me was the chattering spruce forest; ahead lay the most formidable bald I have ever seen—no trees anywhere, their places taken by a towering, impenetrable jungle of steel-branched rhododendron and laurel, wrapping the mountain peak like a hood.

Movement in a rhododendron bush caught my eye. Some animal, about the size of a young child, seemed to be nestled in a matrix of long, shiny leaves and pink blooms. Thinking it to be a cat or a bear cub, I kept still as the mist began its gradual rise. Now I thought my eyes were playing tricks. Reclining lazily within the twisted branches was a naked, motley-colored, flaccid, misshapen creature, entirely beyond my experience or imagination. It seemed perfectly content as it chewed on a cluster of petals. I crept closer. A breeze rolling over the mountain brought me a fragrant, patchouli-like aroma, evidently ascribable to the unnatural being.

It sat there like a large, fat toddler fascinated with a colorful plaything. Its squat head seemed to have partly melted into a puddle of jowls. Two peaceful, lidless eyes and two gnarled structures, possibly ears, adorned its forehead, but I saw neither nose nor hair. Teeth and tongue revealed themselves when the creature's jaw descended in an apparent yawn.

Its two arms and two legs were roughly humanoid in shape but possessed a startling elasticity. The arms stretched out leisurely to half-again their length and dainty fingers picked off flowers, while the flabby torso never moved. The color of the creature's skin varied from albino white above the chest to beige in the mid-section to a deep orange in the lower extremities. The texture of its skin brought to mind a plucked chicken.

This was clearly no terrestrial form of life. I had stumbled upon a dwarfish, aromatic alien.

Protruding from its chest was a most peculiar appendage, attached at its center and resembling an upside-down conch. At first I took it for an ornament because of its metallic sheen, but when the creature batted it idly, it twirled like a lopsided propeller. I saw that it was actually a body part. Its purpose eluded me completely.

I kept watch throughout the morning. Shortly after noon, a second alien, an exact copy of the first, crawled out of the dense foliage. The two of them babbled fervently in a language as inscrutable as the voices of an aviary. Their fragrant aroma intensified. I sensed that they were happy to see each other. After yielding its place in the bush, the first creature disappeared into the thicket. The second arranged itself in their snug little alcove and began chewing a pink blossom. Had I not witnessed the exchange, I would never have guessed it had taken place.

Who are these sweet-smelling Lilliputians and how many inhabit the bald? I saw no more though I watched until dark.

June 5:

After two weeks I have learned a few things about the aliens. First, they station themselves at regular intervals around the bald. In a single day I have counted forty-four. There may be a whole population deep within the bushes. Second, I can now see small variations in their anatomy, reminiscent of the slight differences one finds in identical twins. Could they all be from the same brood? Or have they achieved a remarkable degree of genetic control?

Their skin, which is always fully exposed, seems to be their olfactory organ. Their fragrant scent arises from the shiny appendage on their breast. I would love to examine this conch-shaped organ more closely. If it hasn't a role in mating, I cannot imagine a use for it.

I am still probing for access to the heart of the bald. The massive interwoven shrubs refuse to be violated. After a few yards of pulling, squeezing, and twisting I am too exhausted to go on. If only I could transform myself into one of these wee elastic creatures.

August 10:

Today I finally penetrated to the center of the bald—the fruit of two months of excruciating labor. I have carved out an above-ground tunnel beneath the lowest branches. Access is still difficult, but assured. And my efforts were richly rewarded.

A whole colony of them dwells on a grassy field, the last shrub-free half-acre of the original bald. Approximately two hundred aliens were there; an exact count was impossible. I could not tell differences in gender, but there was a range of sizes; infants and children seemed to be present. Scattered about the field were numerous ceramic-like fragments. I am only guessing but they could be the remains of the vehicle that brought these creatures here.

I found the aliens in a state of extreme torpor. They lay supine in the shade of bushes and hardly stirred. The heat and drought must torment them. Their skin looked dry and scaly, and their limbs had lost their amazing elasticity. Even when I approached within arm's length they were too lethargic to respond.

A new scent—much like hickory smoke—emanated from their breasts. Inhaling this essence, I felt an overwhelming thirst myself. A single urgent thought possessed me.

Returning to my campsite, I took my canteen and stewpot down to the spring, filled them with water, and struggled back up the hill. I crawled through my tunnel and quietly set the pot beside one heat-stricken creature. When he lunged for it, the pot overturned. He vainly tried to save the water, finally burying his jowly face in the sedge and emitting agonized yelps. I hurried back to the spring, refilled the pot, and this time managed to pour some of the water over his parched body. Judging from the sounds he made, it gave him enormous relief.

I went down and up the hill all day fetching water. As word spread throughout the colony, they all dragged themselves across the field for refreshment. By evening they were able to walk and chatter. I tried to communicate with them, but they responded neither to words nor to gestures. When I touched one of them, the whole crowd waddled in terror into the bushes.

They allow me to penetrate their fortress, accept my aid, then shun my attempts to befriend them. They react as instinctively as animals, yet their intelligence cannot be doubted. Have these creatures traveled light-years only to keep aloof? Why won't they trust me?

I've lost my canteen, probably in the tunnel. If it doesn't turn up tomorrow, I'll have to buy another one in town, which means six days wasted. Best to save that errand for the future.

August 20:

Flowers and leaves are their food of choice. They also like beetles, which are slow enough for them to catch. They eat partridgeberries and mushrooms if I set them out. So far I have detected no waste products; their metabolic systems must be extremely efficient.

They use fragments of their spaceship (?) as bowls to collect rain. They bathe two or three times a day, apparently out of urgent necessity.

The children spar and roll in the grass. The adults spend most of their time in the bushes, idly chewing leaves or playing some kind of game with rocks and ceramic chips. Occasionally two adults will separate from the larger group and perform a fascinating dance in which their bodies elongate, intertwine, and quiver amid bursts of squealing and twittering. A strong lilac scent billows up from their breast organs. If I am close enough to inhale it, the most pleasant sensations permeate my body.

October 26:

Since finding the colony I have been troubled by bouts of vertigo. These occur every ten days or so and always catch me unprepared. To avoid fainting I must sit on the ground and focus my eyes intently on an object. Minutes later the ordeal ends, leaving me shaken and confused.

Today I experienced such an attack. Had it not delayed me, I might have prevented a catastrophe, which I shall describe here.

Every day I patrol the entire perimeter of the bald. My rounds begin at dawn and end in mid-afternoon. Having checked all the alien sentries, I crawl through my tunnel to the edge of the field. I spy on the colony until convinced that no new disasters—like last month's incident with the hawk and the infant—have befallen them.

This morning, on the north trail, I began to feel dizzy and immediately lowered myself to the ground. I tried unsuccessfully to focus on something. The distant hills became a spinning blur of autumn color. I lost consciousness. Ten minutes later I awoke, still dazed and wondering what was happening to me.

When I reached the 38th sentry, he was enjoying a catnap, as they frequently do in their tedious posts. Suddenly he snapped awake, and a searing ammoniacal odor filled the air. A volley of angry barking erupted in the woods. I saw that a poacher and his dog had ascended to the edge of the trees and positioned themselves a few yards in front of the alien. The man leveled a shotgun from behind a spruce tree.

Jolted from my own worries, I hurled myself at the protruding gun barrel. The astonished poacher struggled with me for the weapon. It discharged between us with a blast that slammed us both to the ground. We faced each other in a moment of shock and paralysis. With my ragged hair and the hellfire that must have burned in my eyes, I was surely the very portrait of madness. The man scrambled to his feet and fled back through the woods with his dog. I pursued them down the steep slope although in my state of wild alarm I had no idea what to do with them. That issue was abruptly taken out of my hands. They both tumbled onto an outcropping of rock and slid off into bottomless space. The man's scream of terror froze my heart.

Back on the bald I saw that the alien was gone. The shotgun was nowhere in sight. A trail of milky fluid, resembling the hemolymph of an insect and smelling like ammonia, led into the bushes. Nearby I found the shiny scent-organ, ripped from the little one's breast by the buckshot. More of the noisome fluid seeped from its mangled wound. This organ is a remarkable composite. Though it gleams like polished steel, it is more porous and elastic than human flesh. I have preserved it in an airtight plastic container.

The incident with the poacher must not be repeated. I'm not sorry for the man; his kind brings wanton violence to the mountains. I grieve for the helpless sentry, lying dead somewhere or in mortal agony. Here and now I swear an oath to protect the colony from further harm.

November 28:

I have learned how they overwinter. They hibernate in parts of their spaceship, which they cover with mounds of earth and dead leaves. They erect these mounds beneath the bushes.

I myself will spend the winter in an abandoned bat cave on the south face. When the snows come, I must be available if needed.

December 31:

I have developed a theory about the aliens. Their ancestors landed here at least two centuries ago, and the blasts from their ships destroyed the trees on several peaks. Thus were created the balds, which are known to be that old but whose origin has always been a mystery. Survivors of the journey and the landing joined up in the forest. There they lived for years, encountering the Cherokee and the early settlers with results as violent as human nature. (What a shame that we humans, who should be their greeters and hosts, student and teachers, ambassadors of our planet, are feared and distrusted by them.) As new shrubbery covered the balds, the little ones retreated to these safe havens. In all my explorations I have never found signs of these creatures elsewhere. This may be the last surviving colony.

They still face many dangers. When their skin dries out, they become vulnerable to insects. Flies and mosquitoes feast on their white upper bodies, leaving painful blue welts. Every day of summer I must check their rain bowls. I don't know how to protect the children from birds of prey (two infants carried off). And of course there is always the threat of human intrusion. The sound of an airplane causes them no alarm; I have to scare them into the bushes. This problem concerns me greatly.

Did this colony choose to remain on Earth or were they stranded by their brothers? Are they scouts for a larger invasion? What happened to their tools and weapons? Surely a race that achieved space travel must have possessed technological wonders; yet these creatures cannot even produce fire. I think their earthly stay, their confinement on the bald, and possibly inbreeding have caused their minds and bodies to deteriorate over the centuries. Only their scent-organs, marvelous broadcasters of their emotions, remain healthy.

They rebuff all my attempts to communicate. My fellow humans would likely be offended by such discourtesy and treat them as unwelcome immigrants. Cruel men would be spurred on to savagery by their awkwardness and timidity. I must shield the little ones from these perils.

Second Year

January 6:

Another day of light snow. I made it through the tunnel and found their winter cocoons undisturbed. Even their slight movements have ceased. I cannot tell if they're alive, but I maintain hope. I must hike to the cave while the trails are still open.

January 8:

Heavy snow. I cannot leave the cave. Thank God I have plenty of food and firewood. I spent the day reading Muir and Thoreau. The snowy vista is breathtaking. I hope that someday the little ones can appreciate the beauty of this planet.

I had intended to add some poems to my chapbook, but it's gone. It must be lying under snow at the campsite. A pity, for the mountains and my ruminations on the colony inspire me.

(The chapbook, canteen, Swiss Army knife, cans of food—all missing in the last six months. I must keep better track of my things.)

The dizzy spells are milder and less frequent now. My head is clear. The pure, icy air restores my health and invigorates me. But I sorely miss the fragrance of my little ones.

April 3:

They are stirring! The first sleepyheads have risen from their long winter nap and are nibbling dandelions and buttercups. I made sure their rain bowls were full.

April 10:

I counted as carefully as possible: 206. All but four survived. I rejoice! I anoint myself with their essence.

June 20:

Another baby was killed by a hawk. I didn't see it happen but the bird must have dropped the child from the air. The grieving mother bleated and slapped the ground as she clutched the gored remains. Her agony lasted all day and into the night. Eventually several of them dug a hole, buried the child, and crowded around the mother. The whole colony gazed up at the midnight sky and gabbled a somber chant that rose and fell discordantly for over an hour. Though it was gibberish to my ears, I imagined they were singing about a homeland that had only become a legend.

As they mourned, a piney smell arose from their congregation and spread above the field. When it reached my nostrils, a heavy sorrow weighed upon my heart and sapped all my energy. Later, quite bemused and listless, I made my exit. Their effusions overpower me like an addiction. They may be causing my dizzy spells. When I inhale these aromas, I feel emotionally bonded to the colony. Their problems become my obsessions. It has always been my rule to observe the natural world without influencing it; now I cannot resist the impulse to intervene. When the little ones need me, I hasten to their rescue.

July 17:

Today I used my hatchet to cut two slender trees near the bald. Hard work. I dragged them uphill and, one by one, maneuvered them through the tunnel. I am determined to build shelters for the children. If they can learn to play inside them, they should be less vulnerable to the birds. I plan to add three or four trees per day.

August 7:

A setback. While cutting I was overcome by dizziness. I twisted my ankle and fell into a chasm, where I lay unconscious for an hour or so. My vision is still blurred, and it is hard to write. I will have to pace myself more intelligently

August 8:

Better today except for my ankle, which is sore and will not support my weight. One tree harvested, but I couldn't get it uphill. My little ones are okay.

August 22:

Four trees today. I must go further downhill to find the right size. Another dizzy spell, just before supper, and 1 couldn't eat anything.

October 10:

First shelter finished. It is simply a log roof supported on several clusters of logs. I camouflaged it with rhododendron branches. As soon as I withdrew, they all waddled out from the bushes to investigate. They chattered and squealed, and the children tussled playfully under the roof I think they understand its purpose. I tried again to communicate but was totally ignored.

December 6:

I took a chance and left them during their hibernation period. I descended the mountain and rode a bus to the library in Asheville.

Several books on Appalachian history contained anecdotes about goblins and strange woodland odors. To uninformed persons this would be typical mountain folklore, but I am sure it supports my theories.

While in town I had a close call. A spell of vertigo, the worst yet, hit me and 1 passed out. I woke up on a gurney in an emergency room. A doctor and an ambulance driver were talking about me. The doctor asked me questions but I didn't answer. They're not to be trusted. They'd find a way to keep me down and helpless.

My head was throbbing. The doctor probed around my skull, shined a light in my eyes and ears, then went to get someone else. The driver followed him out. I forced myself onto my feet and staggered out of the hospital. Somehow I found my way to the bus station.

I will never abandon my darlings.

Third Year

July 8:

My health continues to ebb. The vertigo leaves me clammy and nauseous, with headaches and double vision. I have no appetite and am nothing but skin and bones. Some days I can hardly move. Yet I do not falter when the little ones need me. I've built them shelters, maintained their water supply during drought, found netting to stop the insects, caught trout in the vain hope of strengthening their bodies with protein. I've guarded their beds in winter and scattered their sentries whenever a poacher or hiker ventured too close. Today another crisis befell the colony. The outcome is still in doubt.

This afternoon they were all in the field. The children were tumbling in and out of the shelters. Suddenly I heard distant engines. The airplane from the south has become a regular menace. It flies over the bald on alternate weeks. Every time it passes I must shoo my angels under cover.

I leaped into the open, shouting and waving my arms. Fleeing from my commotion, one group waddled toward the corner abutting the precipice. A nest of wasps awaited them. The angry villains shot out of the ground and hailed down upon my little ones, mutilating their torsos into purple, suppurating lumps. Fifty victims bleated and writhed in the grass. The ammoniacal stench—their alarm bell—flooded the air. I hobbled across the field, flung netting over them, and took the wrath of the wasps upon myself. My face and arms accumulated a dozen painful stings. The swarming devils chased me back to the tunnel, where I finally eluded them.

Ignoring my own distress, I crawled through and lurched down to the spring. A patch of beebalm grows there. I stuffed the minty weeds into my shirt and pants, clawed my way uphill, and struggled back to the field. For hours I applied poultices to my suffering dear ones. It was futile. All fifty of them died in hideous torment.

I wept and shouted my rage: "Why did this happen? I only wanted to protect them. They cannot survive without me."

Ten yards away the colony gathered to watch. I heard an undercurrent of gurgling voices. Their expressions never change, and I couldn't assess their reactions. I smelled nothing, as if their scent-organs were being suppressed to hide their feelings. Exhausted and ill, I stumbled through them. They retreated before my step, then followed me as far as the tunnel.

"Do you understand what I've done for you?" I cried. "I am your savior!" They only stared. Their faces remained immobile. Not a trace of odor came my way.

July 12:

Today was the first time in four days that I've seen the colony. The disaster with the wasps left me sick at heart as well as in body. I could not stand on my feet. The vertigo would not abate.

This morning I felt well enough to negotiate the tunnel. They have buried the dead, probably at night to escape the wasps. I noticed freshly turned earth near the precipice.

Within the burial ground is a flat, table-sized surface of rock, which I had overlooked until now. It is surrounded by laurel and is safely removed from the wasp nest. There I was surprised to find all the articles I have missed over the years—my canteen, Swiss Army knife, magnifying glass, wool socks, many open and rusted food cans. My chapbook was there with half its pages torn out. A shotgun, most likely the poacher's, had been dissected.

In addition there were tools and implements which looked like relics from the pioneer days, along with Indian arrows and beaded jewelry. Although this discovery supports my theories, it left me mortified. I had forgotten that the little ones are intelligent beings. They have been studying me while I, in my egregious vanity, believed I was studying them. They and their ancestors have been gathering data on humans for perhaps two centuries.

As I sifted through their cache, lidless eyes stared out from the bushes. I heard no sound, caught no scent. They were all around me.

One of them waddled into view, making low, rasping sounds. He held the round edge of his scent-organ, and for some reason this made me think: The time has come. Now we will communicate.

I sat on my haunches. He began to chant the mournful gibberish which I have heard on sad occasions. The others took up the chorus, too. They all stepped out of the bushes, and I was completely surrounded by tremors of sound, escalating to a crescendo. Their leader pointed the tapered end of his scent-organ at me. A jet of liquid shot into my face. I fell backward, blinded, and began coughing and fighting for breath. I thought the caustic oil would dissolve my eyes and lungs. They kept up their dreadful chant as I rolled witlessly on the ground. Then they quit. I could hardly see and I had to strain for every breath. The little ones had disappeared into the bushes. I got to my feet and made for the tunnel.

I have no idea what day it is. My life is ebbing away. When I returned to the colony, they rushed at me, pointing their scent-organs, and I had to flee. They still blame me for the wasp attack. Even after my long devotion to their community, they won't accept me back. I am crushed. I don't want to live. But if I must die on this evil mountain, I will not die alone.

Thus ended Willoughby's journals. Unfortunately they gave no hint about the location of his mountain. Many adventurous souls have searched for it without conclusive results. One hiking party did find some clues, but its members disagreed about their significance.

They found ceramic fragments on what might have been a heath bald. The site had been ravaged by fire, and the verdure was in various stages of recovery. One fellow ventured that Willoughby, in his half-blind, vengeful state, had cremated the aliens and possibly immolated himself at the same time. He insisted that the ceramic shards supported Willoughby's account. But another man argued that lightning fires were well-documented in the Smokies, and no remains of any creature, let alone aliens, had been discovered. Also, if the aliens had stolen Willoughby's equipment—and even his book of poems—why hadn't they taken his journals?

Questions persisted. What if the aliens had escaped the fire and fled to other parts of the wilderness? What if Willoughby's eccentric mind had finally snapped and he'd created a colossal fantasy? The vertigo that plagued him may have been a symptom of his madness. Or was it a symptom of his addiction to the alien scents?

Local historians and naturalists still tell the story of James Willoughby around campfires. They speak of the marvelous scent-organ, supposedly preserved by Willoughby, as if it were the Holy Grail. Hardy adventurers have scoured the hills for it, or for any definitive answers. But the ancient mists of the Great Smoky Mountains know how to keep their secrets.

About the author:

Jeff lives in Columbus, Ohio, close to his two grown children and four grandchildren. He has had several stories published in small-press and college magazines such as *The Sun, Cimarron Review,* and *Louisiana Literature.*

OUR FATHERS
©2015 by Chelle Wotowiec

It was one of the last summers I would spend with my father. We poured our coffee and slipped out the back door of the beach house, leaving Mom on the couch. We made our way down the long porch and onto the sand. I always loved the feeling of the sand on my feet in the mornings. When we first started coming to this same beach twenty years before, the porches went right down to the main sand. During high tide, I would sit on the bottom step and wait for the waves to come in. About ten years ago, though, the county spent a lot of money and added more sand. There was too much property damage. So that morning Dad and I walked down the steps and through the weeds and brush before we reached the main beach. He was picking up fragments of seashells and examining them between his fingertips. We rarely found anything worth saving, but it didn't stop us from looking.

"Check out this one," he said, tossing a shiny purple shell toward me.

It fell short. The sun was rising, leaving the ocean purple and pink and orange.

I reached down and scooped up the shell. It was the shape of a half-moon with ridges reaching from one end to the other. It wasn't the best shell, but I stuck it in my pocket anyway.

* * *

My father's father was a PhD. Horticulture. He was a short man with stocky shoulders who made me wooden rubber-band shooting

47

rifles at Christmastime. That is the grandfather I knew and try to remember. The same grandfather, but a different one all-together, did some terrible things that I only heard about later in life. One story goes that when my father was a boy and forgot to feed the rabbits, Grandpa fed Dad his pet rabbit for dinner but didn't tell him until after the fact. Another story goes that, for whatever reason, Grandpa lost his temper and knocked Dad off a twelve-foot ladder with a two-by-four, leaving him in bed for days.

The first time I saw my dad cry was at my grandfather's funeral. Actually, the funeral hadn't even started yet. We were in the car on the way to the wake and a light turned red. Dad stopped and began sobbing. So much so that he got out of the car and let Mom drive the rest of the way.

* * *

It wasn't until recently that I learned seashells are made of calcium and bones. Creatures created backward—skeleton on the outside—died within the shell and left their bones to be washed ashore.

The air smelled like seawater and early morning sun.

Dad had just turned fifty and I began to feel his age in the tone of his voice and the silver hair lining his ears. His hands were grease-stained, displaying to the world his passion for doctoring manmade machines. As a child, I saw nothing unusual about his black fingernails and dry scaly skin. I assumed it came with age and one day my hands would look the same.

"This is the biggest piece we've found all week," he showed me an eighth of a sand dollar in his grease-lined palm. A few steps ahead of him, I saw a penis drawn in the sand. I hurried ahead while he talked about the bloodlines of the creature.

"There's really not a lot of shells this year," Dad said, catching up with me and taking a quick glance at the mess of sand I'd made.

"I think I read that it has something to do with the phases of the moon."

"Hm." He bent over to pick up a smooth white shell shaped like a side-heavy heart.

I inherited his bone disorder. As he showed me a broken conch on the beach I noticed the bone jutting up from his pointer finger, trying to break through his skin. I looked at my own pointer finger. I was ashamed of my deformity. I grew up with my hands cupped inside long-sleeved shirts year round. My right calf is larger than my left, leaving my legs pale and hidden along with my arms and fingers. On the beach, though, I am content in my bathing suit, my bones jutting freely toward the sun.

Shortly before World War I, a scientist by the name of René Quinton replaced a dog's entire blood supply with seawater. I wanted to tell Dad how I didn't care about science and what we might have thought seawater was capable of doing at the time, but when reading the article my skin stopped breathing and beating as I imagined this dog breathing salt—*being* salt. Then I wondered what kind of father Quinton had.

I didn't want Dad to feel the same way, so instead of mentioning Quinton's experiment to him I asked him if he remembered the time we had found the starfish.

Dad nodded his head as he placed his hand into the pocket of his shorts and let the shell fall in.

We'd been walking down the same beach five years ago when it began to rain. Mom always said she liked the way the rain left the sand behind. In the distance, we saw something fall from a seagull's beak. As we grew closer, Dad scooped it up in his hand. The starfish was red with a tiny center but had only three long legs. *It's breathing*, he'd said, as he flipped it onto its back to show me its center pulsating. Mom, a few steps behind, hurried over to see what the fuss was about.

"Will it survive?" She asked, looking at the creature but not getting too close.

"It's worth a shot," Dad said. Together, the three of us walked waist deep into the water and watched as Dad threw the starfish as far as he could.

* * *

It was Mom's grandfather who found the beach in Oak Island, North Carolina when her father was just a kid. They were looking for a nice beach that was away from the tourists.

One of my favorite memories is of Dad and Mom sitting on the sand with their legs stretched out. The sun was disappearing, leaving those beautiful colors of purple, blue, orange, and red in the sky. Mom's hand was on his leg and they were both laughing. I remember thinking that they were happy. It was the first time I realized the two them didn't seem happy too often.

From behind on my beach towel, I heard Dad tell her about how the Vikings sometimes sent their dead off on boats. He told her that the idea of his body, or whatever was left after death, being sent off to the sea scared him. Besides the fact that he couldn't swim, he said there was something empty about the whole idea. Mom said the ritual was really for the people left behind, not for the dead. The image of their dead drifting off to sea was comforting.

I laughed when Mom promised him she would never send him off into the ocean.

* * *

That last year, Dad and I were back from our seashell hunt a little after breakfast. Mom and Dad sat on the beach reading the newspaper while I stood in the water rinsing and examining the individual shells.

It'd been years since Mom last came to Oak Island with us. She said it was because of work, but I knew it was because she couldn't handle all of the competition. Every woman in a bathing suit made her feel terrible about herself. The island that was once secluded back when her father was just a boy, had been discovered and was more and more populated every year.

This early in the morning, though, there were very few people on the beach other than a few old men and their dogs.

Mom rarely laughed. On the rare occasions when she did laugh, it was usually masked in discomfort—in her eyes. She doesn't fit well. On a train once, at only twelve years old, I remember feeling like Mom was trying to escape her own bones as she sat with her feet tucked beneath the seat, her hands clasped together, and her empty eyes staring into nothingness.

* * *

At eight years old my mom had me crawling through the barn army style searching for the women Dad was hiding; the women he was hiding in the barn. She told me all men were pigs and would always want more than a woman could give them.

My mother's father was crazy. Or at least, that is how I remember him. Mom always blamed the war. She said that it took something from him that he was never able to get back. I didn't know about all of that, though, all I knew was that he would randomly scream at the dinner table. He didn't scream words. He just screamed as loud as he could. Not just once, either. It happened almost every time we had him over. Mom couldn't handle it, so every time he screamed, she screamed and then everyone was screaming and dinner was ruined.

As a ten year old I believed my mother. I was certain that there were women stashed in the barn, living off of rats and cockroaches.

"Don't worry, Mom, I'll find them."

She waited hours for me to return to the house, hoping for proof. But it didn't take me long to realize there wasn't a woman in the barn. I searched it floor to ceiling, spider web to bird nest.

It was when she cried that she made me question my own certainties.

"I know she's in there, Rachel. I *know*." Her face was bloated and her cheeks were cherry red.

"Have you ever seen her?"

"No."

"Then how do you *know*, Mom? I'm telling you, I've looked. I've *really* looked. Everywhere."

"Obviously not good enough."

"No, Mom, I did. Over and over. There is no one there."

"Maybe she hides good."

"Why don't you just ask Dad?"

"I have."

"And?"

"He says I'm being ridiculous."

"You are."

"Whose side are you on?"

* * *

I never knew my parents to be in love. Not the love I have seen in the movies, the backseat of muscle cars, or at county fairs. My parents rarely even kissed or flirted. As a teenager, I was surprised when boys began whispering love notes in my ears. I remember being in the back of an old beater car with a boy who ran his fingers through my hair before he pressed his wet lips against mine. I remember the feeling it ignited in my stomach and the way my skin seemed to beat and breathe as his hand blindly fondled my body while "Gone 'Til November" played on the stereo. The boy told me he was going to drop out of high school and work on a train. I never knew the boy well enough to ask about his father, nor did the thought occur to me at the time. I never associated any of the lust or romance with my parents, and with my parents I associated permanence.

* * *

Eight years ago, I was back home in our large country house.

"You don't think he'll smell it, do you?" I was fourteen years old and without a sense of smell. Another birth defect, but at least this one was invisible.

"No, he won't smell it. Trust me, it'll be fine." Jessie was sixteen and my boyfriend of two and a half months. He was bone thin with bleach-blonde hair. He had a father with a speech impediment and a mother who was never there. Rarely did we talk about these kinds of things, though. It wasn't like that with Jessie.

Jessie lit the bowl and inhaled the smoke deep into his throat. He closed his eyes and pursed his lips before exhaling out the opened window.

"Pass it here, hurry up." Greg, Jessie's younger brother, was built like an RV. His arms combined were bigger than my entire body. Greg told me once that the two of them had been molested. He told me that his father took turns on them. Never penetration, though. He said that his father said he would never do that to them. Then Greg laughed, though, so I wasn't sure what to make of the whole thing. He gestured Jessie to bring the bowl across the room.

"Come over to the window, idiot." I hadn't taken a hit yet and knew better than to let the smoke settle in the walls. I imagined the scent becoming the bones of my basement bedroom: a smoke shell. We would become the slug living and growing inside our shell of pot smoke.

Ten minutes later and all three of us were fried. Jessie had taken the floor fan and aimed it toward the open window. I was lying in bed next to Greg who was rubbing his foot up and down my leg. He sat up and pulled the yellow Mickey Mouse comforter over our bodies.

Footsteps.

"Did you hear that?" Jessie looked over to the bed, and turned off the fan. I was so relieved that Greg had stopped fondling my leg with his dirty foot that I didn't realize the sound of the backdoor closing and the footsteps crossing the dining room, entering the kitchen, and stopping at the top of the stairs leading to my bedroom.

"Rachel!" My father's voice echoed.

"Oh, fuck." I flew up out of bed. My body felt heavy. Heavy, but fast. I looked at Greg and saw that his penis was out of his pants. My body moved faster than my brain could comprehend. "Was this laced?" I thought I whispered.

"I—I don't know." Jessie croaked.

"I thought you said he wouldn't smell it?!"

"He didn't—he couldn't—"

"Rachel!"

"Coming!"

My skin breathed, a similar feeling to that created by the boy in the back of the beater car. Each cell in my body had its own heart and each heart was beating faster than the next.

Something beyond me—not God, hell no, definitely not God—placed my hand on the doorknob, turned it, and I began walking up the stairs. I peeled myself out of the smoke shell and into the real world, into the world where I had a father. *Play sober. Play sober. Play sober. Play sober.* I watched one brown stair turn into the next and into the next and into the next until I felt Dad's presence.

"Rachel, are they smoking pot down there?"

I didn't look at his face. I imagined, if I ever got caught, I could lie. I could play *good* and get myself out of it. A few weeks earlier, Jessie and I had stood in front of my bedroom mirror and practiced playing sober for an hour. *Me? I'm not stoned. No. You're crazy!* I laughed at my ridiculous reflection and Jessie practiced keeping a straight face. But now there was nothing funny about it and knew I couldn't lie. I couldn't speak. He asked again. Whatever it was that made me turn the doorknob now made me nod my head. I was peeling the seashell from my skin and giving it to Dad to keep.

Silence.

I realized I wasn't wearing shoes. When had I taken off my shoes? Silence.

"You too?" His voice was impregnated.

Silence.

"Look at me."

I was in control now, and there was no way I was going to lift my head.

Silence. And then tears hit the floor; his or mine, I wasn't sure.

* * *

I had almost finished deciding which shells would make it back into the beach house and which ones I would secretly leave behind when the boy's scream for help pierced our silence. I looked to my right and saw nothing. To my left, and saw nothing. Both Mom and Dad had dropped their papers and were looking out into the sea. And then Dad was running as fast as he could straight into the water. That's when I saw him—a young boy no older than six or seven, floating head down about fifty feet from where I stood.

"He can't swim!" My mother screamed. I knew she was referring to Dad, not the boy. For a moment, I was surprised she knew that about him.

The boy's father, a tall skinny redheaded man who appeared to be in his early twenties, came running from the beach house next to ours.

"Jimmy!" he screamed. There were circles under the man's eyes and I could see the anger in his face.

* * *

"Wake up." Mom's hand rubbed my forehead. It was the day after Dad had caught me smoking pot in the basement.

I kept my eyes closed, hoping she would think I was still asleep.

54

"Honey, wake up. We're leaving in fifteen minutes."

"Where?"

"To go hiking at Mohican."

"What? Why?"

"It's your father's idea."

The seventy-six minute drive felt like I was back with Mom on the old couch, with the cushions covered in barns and horses, watching *The Ten Commandments* in complete silence. Except now, my stomach hurt every time Dad cleared his throat.

The entire day, I waited for Dad to out me to Mom and declare my punishment. He rarely looked at me, but when he did it was to point out an orange newt or a tree that didn't grow back at home.

That was the first time our relationship acknowledged the unspoken agreement it had taken. Maybe it had been there all along. Maybe even when I was a child searching for his make believe mistress.

* * *

The red headed man stood helplessly on the beach as he watched Dad grow closer to his boy.

And then Mom was in the water.

Dad looked no bigger than an ant. Mom swam toward him, shrinking just like the boy and Dad. Far out, their limbs entangled, Mom and Dad got the boy to float. His dad began to cry and talk to God as I waited patiently for time to pick back up.

The boy was limp as Dad finally dragged his body onto the sand. The boy, the poor boy, was bloated and blue. He looked more like a fish than a boy. Or death.

When the boy finally began to breathe, I thought about that starfish and how maybe it all came back around after all.

About the author:

Michelle has found herself living and teaching English in Phoenix, Arizona. She often finds herself on the couch wondering which choices led her to this stage in life, when only two years ago she was waiting tables in Cleveland. She thinks about the important points in life: Her first kiss on the top of a rocket slide, her first love wearing baggy Jencos in the hallways of a junior high school in Sullivan, Ohio, her first heartbreak on her sister's green and white plaid futon, sad country songs playing from the boombox. She remembers the enlightening lessons her father showed her through his treatment of the homeless man he provided shelter for in the trailer out back behind the cornfield and acknowledges that it is him she often thinks about when she imagines what it is to be a genuinely caring person. She remembers the first moment she acknowledged the power of a smile and a buying into the belief of optimism. True optimism. The type of optimism that tells her things aren't so bad and people are good. She thinks about all of these things and is brought back to her reality of Phoenix, Arizona by her cat, Kissy Kit, climbing onto her shoulders and purring in her ears.

From the relationship the narrator has with her father, the relationship between her parents, to the young boy taken out to sea, "Our Fathers" looks at the human condition and the different relationships we build with those around us and what, if anything, they mean.

Michelle feels so privileged to have the opportunity to share her writing yet again with Scribes Valley Publishing. She thanks her mother, father, sister, and friends for the inspiration to continue the journey in her love of writing.

Finally, she thanks you for reading.

SUSTAINED PRESSURE
©2015 by Joyce Munro

> Operation Rolling Thunder continues to drop tons of bombs on North Vietnam daily. The President has vowed to continue sustained pressure indefinitely.
> --*United Press International, Statesville Journal, March 16, 1966, page 1*

Every time Lois walked into Claire's dorm room, her eyes went straight to the photograph on Claire's desk. Father and mother, son and daughter—like a double set of twins—with their model-perfect faces and honey-blonde hair. The camera caught them strolling, arms linked, long legs taking them straight to the sun. Lois got a lump in her throat when she looked at them.

Compared with the Taylor family, Lois's family pictures were like "before" snaps in a magazine article about beauty makeovers. Her family was a quarrelsome bunch and that's what the camera exposed—uncomfortable smiles, standing askew to keep from touching. All of them wore glasses so the flash made white streaks across their eyes. And as soon as the photographer was finished, they went right back to bickering.

Lois assumed anyone who attended a college with *Bible* for its middle name came from families like hers: they loved Jesus, just not each other that much. But when she first arrived on campus, she was startled to see lots of happy students, not sourpusses. She thought they were a little too nonchalant to be attending Bible college. After all, the college's motto made it clear: *We're here on business for the King.*

Whenever they took breaks from studying the King's business, Lois saw them mingling, linking arms, laughing as they walked across the Commons.

Her family did a lot of jabbing but never linked arms, so the day she saw the Taylor family for the first time, she went back to her room, took her family photo—the one made at Olan Mills—and shoved it in her dresser drawer.

Lois couldn't get enough of the Taylors looks. Especially Claire's brother. All through freshman year, she wished Claire's roommate would get homesick and leave. Then she could move in and fall asleep every night looking at him. It didn't happen that way.

* * *

After a year's worth of running in and out of Claire's room with excuses just to glimpse the blonde god, Lois actually met him—the weekend she returned for sophomore year. She was lugging a suitcase and duffle bag to her dorm when he strolled toward her, tall and glistening and gorgeous, the photo come to life, only his mop of hair had been cut short, military style. She cringed, hoping he would walk past her, what with her hair not teased, glasses falling off her nose, and arms covered with mosquito bites. But he stopped. And he spoke. To her.

"Here, let me handle those."

All she could do was blink at him and gulp air. She stupidly pointed the way and they started up the hot stairwell. He went a step behind her. She could feel his huffing and puffing against her skirt and it made her weak-kneed.

When she opened the door to her room, he brushed against her—she would have felt it, except she had on a padded bra. He hefted her bags onto the bed, then stood in the middle of the room shaking his muscles loose. A drop of his sweat hit her forearm—she let it sit there. He gave her a lopsided grin and he spoke to her a second time.

"You and me gotta take a break."

She almost peed in her panties.

They ended up sharing a Coke from the machine in the basement. He only had one quarter, so they took turns drinking from the same bottle. Her fingers laced with his as they passed the bottle between them and she didn't wipe off the rim each time she held it to her mouth.

He leaned against the wall and told her about driving non-stop from Chicago, just to say goodbye to Claire. He was shipping out. He expected to get to Vietnam this time instead of lazing on the base in Okinawa. The only thing he worried about was how he was going to keep the grunts from making him walk point. She didn't ask him what he meant, just nodded like she knew all about it. He asked her to look in on Claire now and then, because being at a Bible college was hard for her. She told him she'd be happy to. And he spoke to her one last time:

"Break's over. I gotta go."

He put the empty bottle on the floor. Then he flexed his muscles and leaned toward her. He smelled like the gym at Lois's old high school when sweaty boys competed for most sit-ups. She thought he was going to kiss her and it was too late to take off her glasses. But he just tapped her chin with a wet finger and left her standing there, breathless.

* * *

For a whole year, Lois had gazed at his image, but that didn't prepare her for the touch and smell of him that scorching August day. In the back of her notebook, she started writing his name with fancy flourishes and sketched his torso and recorded his vital information, which she had to drag out of Claire. By October, he filled twelve pages.

Sometimes Claire read his latest letter out loud and Lois would race back to her room and write down things he said:

> *I've walked point several times no problem. The VC are firing rockets night after night so no one can get any sleep. I've started smoking. Thank God our platoon hasn't been fired on directly. This constant tension is beginning to get to me. C-rations are making us sick. Send real food!*

The first Saturday in December, Lois helped Claire pack a box for him—canned ham, dried fruit, cookies, and a mini plastic Christmas tree with candy canes. Lois wanted to give him something expensive, something he could treasure always, something that would link him to her. But after shopping for three weeks, she gave up. She thought about giving him her photo from freshman year, except she looked pathetic. She started writing a passionate letter, tore it up, and wrote a nice Christian girl note: *Hope you stay safe...I pray for you every night...enjoy the real food...Merry Christmas...yours truly.* She added a long P.S.—verses from Psalm 91 about not being afraid of terror in the night and angels guarding him, keeping him safe from hidden danger. She put her note and five packs of cherry Kool-Aid in an envelope and gave it to Claire.

After the holidays, Lois kept hoping he would mention her in his letters to Claire. Or, better yet, write her back. He didn't. Her carefully scripted memories of their fingers laced together, his sweat sizzling her flesh, his face almost touching hers, and a sticky Coke bottle were all she had of him.

* * *

On an evening during spring midterms, Lois was standing at Claire's desk, running her finger around the silver frame and over his face, when she heard Claire's roommate behind her.

"Well, Claire-roomie, are you ready to practice your testimony? We gotta get Lois back to her room without anybody noticing."

It was the middle of study hours--a risky time for Lois to visit another dorm room. All over Central Hall, girls were hunched over their maple desks, the position for perceiving the theological difference between *eros* and *agape* from mimeographed class outlines. Rules said they could be in the library or in their own rooms. But because testimonies had to be memorized and because Claire—*his* sister—wanted to practice, Lois was breaking rules. In Dr. Howard's class, eight o'clock Tuesday morning, four students were scheduled to speak about how they met Jesus and their plans for full-time Christian service. One of the four was Claire and she wanted Lois and Shelley to time her—Dr. Howard limited testimonies to three minutes.

"All right. Let's do this."

Claire glided to the dresser. Her shiny green robe and satin slippers were nothing like the cover-ups and fuzzy scuffs everyone else wore in the dorm. She was a Queen Esther ready to hold court, the star of one of those late-night movies Lois and her mother used to watch on TV.

"Okay, Shelley, you and Lois sit there." Claire pointed to her bed. "Here goes." She put her right hand in the placket of her robe and raised her chin.

"My fellow students, my name is Claire Augusta Taylor. I was born in Chicago, Illinois and I come from a good Christian family. I am here today because I decided this fine Bible college is where I will finally get my life straight. Actually, my Dad decided for me after my brush with the law. He calls me from somewhere in France at four in the morning and says, '*Salut mon,* pet, I've decided that Hillmont is where God will change your life. It's the right place with the right rules for you. I've prayed about it and your mother agrees—Hillmont is where we are sending you. God loves you and so do I. *Adieu*, pet.'"

Claire slammed an imaginary phone on the dresser.

"That was that and here I am! Now where was I?" She picked up a brass bell and rang it in time with her words. "When I was a teen, I was away from the Lord. My life was kinda blah, I was totally bored. Tarnished and cracked up and rung out so hard, every sound I tried to make was marred, marred, marred."

She grinned and batted her eyes furiously.

Lois and Shelley started to laugh.

Claire shushed them and rang the bell again. "Then I felt ashamed and got it right with the Lord. Now my life is really sharp, like a great big sword. You can believe me, 'cause I'm telling ya true. Today I'm a'ringin' and this is what's new. If I sound like men or angels, but I don't got love, then brassy, brassy, clashy, clashy, *tough, tough, tough!*"

She rang the bell hard, then set it down. "And now that our sophomore year is coming to a close, I'd like to sing a hymn."

She cleared her throat and crooned: "Should auld acquaintance be forgot and never brought to mind..." She sang the words she knew, hummed the rest, sashaying around the room, her long, bare legs flinging her robe open.

"Now how's that for a genuine testimony?"

Lois and Shelley laughed so hard, they fell to the floor and knocked their heads together.

"Ahem..." They didn't hear the door open. A girl of substantial size, buttoned up in a blue seersucker robe, stood in the doorway.

In a hushed voice, she said, "Claire, I know you don't mean to be flippant, but I just wish your testimony was genuine like my testimony is. I'm just going to pray that the Lord will lay it on your heart. Lois, it's study hours and we're not supposed to be out of our rooms. I just need you to stop by and see me for a minute."

The girl smiled and shuffled away.

They looked at the empty doorway and amusement drained from their faces.

"Just, just, just. I *just* thought my testimony needed jazzing up," Claire said. "It *just* needs something." She leaned out the door and stuck her tongue out. "Do you know how many times I've written this? Over and over and *over*. Dozens of testimonies roll around in my head, none of them true. It's so *fake!* I don't *want* to stand in front of class and give a testimony. There's too much going on in the world to spend time on *this* crap. I...*just*...*don't*...*care!*" Claire yelled to the absent floor leader.

Care echoed down the hallway. She slammed the door and beat her fist against it.

Lois gulped and looked at Claire. "Well I guess we shouldn't...be disrespectful of some things."

"Oh really? I disrespect a lot of things. It's *you* who would never be disre*spectful.*" Claire picked up a brush and attacked her hair. "You are so...so...*dull!* Didn't even want to break study hours tonight, Miss Rulekeeper!" She spit words through clenched teeth. "I know exactly what *your* testimony is. You were saved by his blood at a tender age. *Hallelujah!* Baptized by his spirit. *Amen!* Sanctified by obeying *all* the rules. *Praise Jesus!*"

Claire's face was turning purple.

"And soon you'll be the wife of a nobody Bible translator on some far away island where skin is tan...and...and clothes are nil. Gonna win you a couple of souls for *Jesus* in twenty years' time and never *ever* raise enough money to come home on furlough, so you'll never *ever* see your family again because you'll be *dyin'* to serve the Lord! Dying to serve the Lord! Ha! That's a laugh. There's a war going on over there and guys really are getting killed. They're coming home in body bags, for Christ's sake! Ship 'em over, ship 'em back. My brother's gonna come home in a bag—I just know he is—he's been missing for so.... *Oh, hell! Tes*t*imony, Piss*timony!*"

She turned and threw her brush at the dresser. A can of hair spray fell to the floor.

Lois and Shelley flinched. Claire picked up her jewelry box and threw it; then coffee cup, lipstick, razor, contact case, flashlight, apple.

The three girls stared at Claire's belongings scattered on the rug.

"Well, roomie, are we cleaning off our dresser?" Shelley asked.

"No, luv, just being disrespectful." Claire turned to Lois. "And *you*, Miss Dullsville, don't you *ever* ask me another question about him again! *Never!*"

She grabbed the razor and flashlight and ran out of the room.

Lois and Shelley sat there, stunned. Finally Lois stood. She picked up the hair spray and set it on the dresser...scooped the jewelry into the box and put it back...and the cup and the lipstick and the contact case. Nothing was damaged except the apple. She tossed it in the trash can.

"Sorry," Shelley muttered.

Lois drew a deep breath. "Is he really missing?"

"Don't you know? It's been three weeks. I thought she told you," Shelley said.

Lois didn't answer. She took the photograph from Claire's desk and walked out of the room.

At the end of the hall, she stopped at the stairwell window. From there she could look toward the one spot that reminded her of home. Dense woods, ending abruptly at cliffs, maybe half a mile away. Below the cliffs, a river jammed with huge rocks—dramatic terrain compared to the flat land of campus. The river, often swollen after thunderstorms, was off-limits to students.

On a warm evening last October, she had skipped supper and

hiked to the edge of the cliffs. She couldn't bear to go farther; the cliffs were covered with thick slimy vines and the noise of rushing water down below was terrifying. As the light faded, she headed back to the dorm. Occasionally, she would pause by the window and wish she had made it down to the river where she could relive that day with him.

This time, she didn't really look out the window, just stared and hugged the picture close to her chest. All she could see was her horrified expression reflected back in the glass. Then something shimmered out there. A long-legged figure, arms covered in billowing green, like wings, running into the woods. Lois watched until it was too dark.

She sank to the top step and leaned against the railing. In the red glow of the exit sign, she memorized the face of Claire's brother. Unruly blonde hair, a small scar on his forehead she hadn't noticed before, arched eyebrows, tender eyes—so blue, she wondered if he was wearing contacts, straight nose, perfect teeth...

A voice began to sing in her head, soft and slow. *"Should auld acquaintance be forgot and never brought to mind..."*

New words came to her and the voice sang on, stronger and louder: *"We two have drunk our fill of Coke our fingers did entwine, but we will never meet again and you will not be mine. For auld lang syne, my dear..."*

She wanted to keep the song going but she couldn't think of any more words. And the lone sad voice was getting drowned out by a bunch of rowdy drunks garbling the words off key. It made her temples throb. She wanted sentimental, not raucous. Squeezing her eyes tight, she stopped the song.

She raised the photo to her lips and kissed his face. Then, with a languid backhand motion her tennis instructor would have been astonished to see, she sailed the photo over the railing. It ricocheted down three flights of stairs, showering the air with shards of glass, on its way toward the Coke machine.

About the author:

Joyce spent her career in academia, where her writing consisted of scholarly documents suitable for pedagogues and professional students living in Ivory Towers. Now she writes stories for anyone living anywhere, about a college with Bible for its middle name during a time of war (with a nod to Shirley Nelson).

LEEWARD
©2015 by Simone Hanson

The sound of hammering out in the barn woke her. The strikes were loud and they carried sharply in the thin, cold air, but did not startle her. Four mornings in a row now he had gotten up early, within the light of dawn, to work on his new boat. She lay there in the bed, getting her eyes to focus on the white paint of the ceiling, dull gray in this dark morning light. He worried her, what with his excitement over this new boat; his feverish anticipation of finishing it.

A whole career full of boats, and this was his last one, he said. He promised. He wasn't going to sell it, either. This one he wanted to keep for himself, to row around in when he finished it. At his age.

She had to stop thinking. It was time to get up. She had to pack, double-check her flight, and call her daughter, though she was sure Lily wouldn't be up for hours yet. Her daughter was never an early riser.

She'd get her errands done first, then call. She wanted to shop, pick up a few things for him to eat while she was gone. She needed to clean the house, do his laundry. All the things that must be done before you take a long trip. But it was warm in the bed, and the sound of hammer against copper nails played with a steadiness that became a rhythm. Then a miss. Hammer thudding against wood. She pulled back the comforter and swung her legs over the side of the bed and stood. She swayed as she started walking, arrhythmic.

The bathroom floor was cold. It was an unusual cold, a kind that hurt. It felt as though her feet were made of glass and each step forward threatened to break them. She stood in the bathroom for a minute, tile floor threatening to crystalize her feet, wondering what to do first. That was the trouble when you had a lot to do: you had to decide what to do first, then what to do next, and then what to do after that. It turned the day into a series of chores. She couldn't remember when she had started to feel this way, to feel the difficulty in every little thing. It didn't matter now. *Move forward*, she told herself. *Just move forward.*

She thought about getting a cup of tea first, but that would mean going all the way down to the kitchen and then having to climb back up the stairs. It seemed like a waste of time and effort—things she couldn't afford to waste at this point. She'd shower and get dressed quickly and then pack her bag. She'd drag it downstairs herself, she could still do that. Then she could have her cup of tea.

Some people, they needed a cup of coffee first thing in the morning; couldn't function without it, they'd say. That's the way Lily was ever since high school. Maybe it wasn't the best thing for a teenager, but Lily had always hated getting up early for school. It was torture, she'd say. She'd begged her parents to let her drink a cup of coffee in the morning, told them tea wasn't strong enough for her. They hid their smiles when she grimaced at the bitter taste. Their girl. The house had always smelled good, though, at the start of each day.

She wondered if Lily still had that desire for a cup of coffee first thing in the morning. Probably, it was a firm habit by now, she imagined. Well, she'd find out for sure soon enough. She started to feel excited for her trip.

But she was cold, too cold to stand here. She'd sit back on the bed, just for a minute. These days she felt colder and colder all the time. She wondered how her husband could be out there so early each morning, working in the unheated barn. Why was he so tied to this boat?

Tied. That's what he'd been saying. It came back to her slowly, the conversation they'd had the night before. At supper time. What had they had for supper last night? Bisque? Something warm and rich, she remembered that much. He kept talking about how good it was, and he hadn't said it absently. He'd really enjoyed it, she could tell and it made her happy now that she had taken the time to make it for him. And his new boat, he kept talking about the red row boat he was building, a new design. He hadn't had a new design in decades. Not that a row boat was anything original. A dory, he said it was, only on a smaller scale, something he could row around in easily. He was done with outboards, he'd said. His hands didn't grip so well anymore and the engines were hard for him to start. So how did he intend to use an oar, she'd asked him, if his hands weren't working so well? *If you can wave a stick, you can move an oar*, he'd answered. She pictured his hands, the claws they were becoming, and it gripped her heart, the vision of him in his little boat.

When he was done with it, he was going to tie it to the boat hitch. Take it with him everywhere he went. That way, he'd say, when he found the right body of water, he'd be ready. It worried her, the childishness of it all. A red row boat. Dragging it behind him like a child pulling a toy.

He'd put his arms around her waist after they'd eaten, while she stood at the sink washing up, and he'd sung the song. They were reflected, the two of them, in the kitchen window. Their faces were devoid of color, as though they were just shadows of other people looking in at them. They swayed slightly. *Row row row your boat, gently down the stream.* His soft voice, just above a whisper, floated past her. Then all around her. She looked at their reflection again, steam from the hot water wavering before the glass, their image fogged. A trick of her eye, and she saw them younger, Lily with them.

They used to sing it all the time, that absurd song, when Lily was little. She was one of those children who didn't get tired of things easily. Three parts, beginning after each other. They'd sing it over and over, not stopping until one of them lost their place and accidentally started singing along with another. Sometimes they'd sing it through a few times before realizing they had reduced the song to two parts instead of three and then Lily, always laughing, would make them stop and start again.

His arms locked around her, he'd rocked gently back and forth as he sang, his voice breaking almost as soon as he started to sing, crying. She worried so much about him. She shouldn't be leaving him now, to go on this trip to see Lily. But he'd told her to go, that it had been so long since either of them had seen her. They both missed her. "Come with me," she'd said, when she'd first starting planning the trip. "This is ridiculous, why don't we both go? We should both go."

"Let me finish my boat," he'd said. "Then I'll come. Let me find some water. I'll have the boat with me." He smiled at her. "I'll go by sea." She told him she didn't appreciate his foolishness.

She would talk to Lily about it, she'd tell her it was time to think about the future. Yes, even old people have futures, she'd have to tell her. She was still such a child, Lily was. Still in that realm of the young when it's too soon to think about the end of things. Or maybe it was because she took after her father, always so young, in a way.

Your father has a future, she'd have to tell her, and it's coming fast. And the form of it is not pretty. I may need your help at some point. I'll need your help picking out a place where we can put him. She didn't want to think about it. She would put off thinking about it for the moment. She would get dressed and then she'd pack her bag. But first she would sit here, just for a minute, on the bed. Catch her breath before moving again.

* * *

Frank Lancaster worked on his boat out in the cold barn until the ache in his hands forced him to stop. He put away his tools and rubbed his hands together, though he couldn't hope to generate enough friction to spark even a little warmth. He walked the worn out path from the barn to the house, hands in his coat pockets, and went inside.

The house was quiet. He stood for a moment, checking to see if the stillness would last, and when it did, he put two mugs of water in the microwave oven and set the timer for a minute, ten seconds and watched the cups circle around and around until they were hot enough. He set them down on the counter, holding each by their handles. His hands were big and he looked awkward holding the cups that way, like a giant at a tea party, but they were too hot to hold in his hands properly. He dropped a teabag into each cup, waited until they had started to sink into the water before he went upstairs to see if his wife was awake.

In the bedroom, he found her sitting on the edge of the bed. She was still in her nightgown, the long one, and she had it twisted around her legs. If she stood up she might fall. Her hands were in her lap, the fingers of her right hand twisting the bands on her ring finger: the engagement and wedding rings she'd had for almost fifty years now, the sapphire ring she'd had almost as long, and the fourth one, an anniversary band he'd given her. He couldn't remember quite when he'd done that. Years did not separate themselves neatly in his mind. His life was divided by events. And eventualities.

"What's wrong?" he asked her. He sat down next to her on the bed and took both her hands in his. She slipped one hand onto her lap, let him hold her other one.

"It's the strangest thing," she told him. "Can you imagine? I don't know what to pack. I can't even find a pair of shoes that match." She laughed a little and then told him she wasn't fooling. She could not find a single outfit, nothing went together. "I'll look like a homeless person when I get there," she said.

He laughed softly at her.

"No, I'm serious," she said. "How have I gone so long with nothing to wear?" There were tears brimming her eyes. She blinked and broke them apart, fragments clinging to her eyelashes. The fingers of her free hand clenched tightly. She would leave marks in her palm, he thought.

It was the idea of this trip. She'd gotten the idea in her head that she could make a trip to see Lily, and that she could do it alone if he didn't want to go with her. It was an idea a long time coming. He'd humored her at first, telling her he'd go with her just as soon as he finished the new boat. She'd accused him of taking a long time on purpose, so he had started getting up with the first light to prove to her that he would finish it as quickly as he could. He tried to joke with her, to get her to focus on something besides her obsession with this trip, but her patience was gone—it had been thinning for years and now it was worn down to just a fragile thread. His jokes threatened her now. He couldn't blame her; it had been so long since either of them had seen their girl.

He wanted to go, too. He really did.

"How about if you get back in bed," he said gently. He helped her to lean back toward the pillows. She struggled and told him no, that she couldn't lie back down. There was too much for her to do before her flight. "I wanted to run to the store for you, to get you a few things. I'll be gone a while, you know. What are you going to eat?"

"I'll be all right," he told her. "I can fend for myself."

He swung her legs up onto the bed. "Your legs are cold," he said. His voice was nervous. "And your feet are ice. Come on, back under the covers now."

"Not ice," she said.

He couldn't hear her, she spoke too softly. "What did you say?" he asked her. He leaned close to her.

"I said my feet aren't ice. They're glass. Brittle glass. I thought they were going to break just now, when I was in the bathroom."

"I know how that is," he said. "I know all about that." He pulled the comforter gently over her, making sure her feet were covered. "You rest now. There's still plenty of time." He brushed her hair back from her face. When had her dark hair turned this brilliant white? Her face was unlined, but somehow she still looked frail. And her eyes, they didn't have that bright, questioning look they'd always had.

By their age, most questions had been answered. Though not all of them. Not the *why* of everything. Why did this thing happen? Why to us? It didn't matter now. They had made it. They had moved forward. Look at how far they had come.

He took her hand again, told her everything was all right and that she should try to get a little more sleep. It was still so early.

She'd see Lily soon enough. They both would. Lily wasn't going anywhere—she hadn't in a very long time now. And when his wife and child were together again, well, he couldn't even imagine it. To see Lily again, unbroken. To see her face uncracked. Skin whole.

He ran his fingers across his wife's face, her eyes now closed. She was warm and breathing. She wouldn't see Lily today. But soon, soon she would. And he wouldn't be far behind her. He'd get that boat finished. He was close to pounding in the last shining copper nail. He'd put the finishing touches on it, paint it and then give it a name. That's all he had left to do now. He'd find water somewhere near, a new place. He'd put in and row.

About the author:

Simone Hanson is thrilled to have her third short story published by Scribes Valley. When not procrastinating, she is at work on her second novel. She now has an agent, so with any luck one of her books may be in print one day. She lives in Roswell, Georgia with her husband and two of their three children. The oldest is now living in Athens, Georgia where he is having a lot of fun at college. Hopefully not too much fun.

SAFE ON AN ERROR
©2015 by Herb Wakeford

Tuesday afternoons at Sam's Tavern and Sports Bar are usually quiet, which allows me to trade baseball trivia with Sam and rearrange the universe from the comfort of a padded bar stool. On one such Tuesday this past May, I was downing the remains of my second Michelob when the honey-blonde walked in. Until then, the best-looking woman in the place was a short redhead who looked about six months pregnant, so Honey drew the immediate attention of all seven of the male customers, including me.

Understand, now, that I am what is euphemistically called a "happily married man," a term that Sam derides as the ultimate oxymoron. But then Sam writes three alimony checks every month. Nonetheless, I observed discreetly as Honey scanned the room and then slipped her svelte twenty-something body into a booth near the door. Sam, being the gentleman that he is, attended there promptly. He returned quickly, said "Classy," and mixed her a Manhattan.

Sam delivered the drink and came back smiling like the proverbial Cheshire cat. "Do you know her, Jake? She says you look familiar."

"You're kidding, right?" But I looked her way again, just to be sure. She was leaning back in the booth, sipping her drink and watching two guys jostle Sam's vintage pinball machine. "No, Sam, I think I'd remember someone like that."

"Me too," he replied wistfully.

I switched to a Heineken and we reminisced about old girlfriends

75

and ex-wives for a few minutes. We noted sagely that young women change their appearance more than men, so I gave Honey another look. One of the pinball guys was at her booth, likely trying his best pickup line. She let the conversation run a bit, but apparently didn't invite him to join her in the booth—or anywhere else—so he ambled back to the pinball contest. She looked towards me briefly, and then at Sam. She raised her glass and tapped it. He nodded and mixed her another drink.

"If you're still wondering," he teased, "you could go over and introduce yourself. I'll let you take this to her…on the house, even." Sam was grinning like a fool at this point, probably because he could see that I was getting rattled, so I accepted his challenge.

"Hi. I'm Jake Fowler. Sam says you think I look familiar. Did you really say that or is he just messing with me again?"

Honey laughed. "Yes, I really did say that." Her eyes searched my face for a moment. "Did you ever play pro baseball here in Durham, a few years ago maybe?"

"Well, yes…"

"Oh, good. I'm trying to track down some former Bulls players. I was at the Park earlier today and they're putting together a roster of the '99 team for me…"

The '99 team? Uh-oh.

"… but in the meantime they suggested I check the nearby sports bars where some of those guys still hang out. Were you here around that time? Do you remember this?" She handed me a well-worn clipping from The Durham Herald, September 8, 1999:

BULLS PLAYER KILLED IN CAR-TRUCK COLLISION
   Ted Kelly, 22, star pitcher for the Durham Bulls, was killed about 11 PM Monday when his British sports car collided head-on with a Lighthouse Beverage delivery truck on Highway 98 East. The truck driver, Gus Wilson, 55, also died in the crash. There were no passengers in either vehicle and no witnesses to the event.

   "Our entire ball club is devastated by this tragic news," said Bulls' general manager Zeke Gerard. "Ted was a fine young

man and a talented athlete with a bright future."

No specific cause for the collision has yet been determined, but preliminary police reports suggest that the truck may have drifted over the center line of the two-lane highway. A spokesman for Lighthouse, however, stated that they believe their driver was not at fault.

Kelly's nearest relative is a teen-age sister, Barbara, who lives with their aunt and uncle in Roanoke, Virginia. Wilson's wife, Paula, lives in Durham. Neither family could be reached for comment.

"Yeah, I remember that…now. One of those awful things that just don't make any sense. And Kelly was a helluva ballplayer."

Her face lit up. "Did you know him, Jake? I'm his sister, Barbara."

Omigod! Babs Kelly, the skinny kid who hung around the ballpark all that summer.

"Please sit down," she continued, "I want to ask you about Ted. Did you know him well?"

"No, not personally. See, when I said I'd played here in Durham I meant that, uh, literally. I was with the Charlotte Sox then, in the same division as the Bulls, so we played a lot of games here." *Half-truths can protect you, sometimes.*

"Oh. Did you know any of the other Bulls players from that year—Bobby Kirk, Joe Francona, Jimmy Jackson, Garcia, any of them?—or where they might be now? I need to find out…well, it's a long story, and kind of complicated, so…"

The ever-observant Sam, bless him, appeared at that point with a fresh Heineken for me. I took a long swig and nestled the cold bottle into my clammy palms. "That's OK. Go ahead," I said, and waited to hear a story I already knew, but was in no hurry to revisit.

"Ted called me about suppertime that evening—Labor Day 1999. The Bulls' season was over and they hadn't made the playoffs, so we were expecting him home the next day. But he said, 'Babs, I'm going to The Show! Coach Davis told me and Joe to stick around for a couple of days because they might need us in Tampa. Can you believe it?' I was so happy for him. He was my big brother, my hero…"

I know. From my frequent position at third base that summer, I saw you in the family boxes behind the Bulls' dugout, cheering us on and keeping neat little scorecards. Except the games Ted pitched, when you chewed the scorecard into a soggy mess.

"…then my Aunt Rose—she and Uncle Fred raised us after our parents died—woke me about midnight and said, 'Darlin', we got some real bad news.' And then we all cried for a long time."

Barbara sipped her drink again and I took a deep breath.

"And now?" I asked.

"Now," she replied with determination, "now I'm here to be sure that the people responsible for Ted's death are held accountable, and to keep them from trashing his reputation. As this news clip says, the police did think that the truck driver caused the accident. Probably fell asleep coming back from a long delivery run that day. His company denied that, of course, so we had to sue them for Ted's wrongful death. The case has dragged out for years now, partly because I was still a minor then and partly because it's been difficult to say what Ted's so-called 'earnings potential' was, since he didn't have a major league contract at the time. We thought we finally had an agreement last year, but then Lighthouse was bought out by another company—Tri-State—and *their* lawyers got into it. Now they're saying that Ted was drunk that night—or on drugs—and that *he* caused the wreck."

"How can they say that now, Barbara? There was no such evidence at the time…uh, was there?"

"No, none at all. But Tri-State claims to have two guys from that Bulls team who will testify against us. So now it's not just about the money, Jake, it's about Ted himself. I can't let anyone do that to him! I have to find some of Ted's other teammates who…who know the truth about him."

"I'm sure you can. When you get that roster from the Bulls office, show it to Sam. He's had this place for a long time, and he might know where some of those guys are. I'm sorry I can't be much help myself, but...."

"That's OK. Just in case you think of something later, though, let me give you my number. I'm staying with a friend in Chapel Hill." She pulled a business card from her purse and scribbled a number on it. The card said:

Virginia Department of Social Services
Roanoke, Virginia
Barbara L. Kelly, B.A., Counselor

"That's what you do? Counseling?"

"Yeah, with kids mostly. Ted and I grew up in a good, loving family, but a lot of kids nowadays aren't that lucky. So I try to help, and I love my job. What about you, Jake? Did you make it to the majors?"

"No, not even close, really. I didn't have your brother's kind of ability."

"So what are you doing now?"

"I'm a stix-tech."

"A what?" she grinned.

"Statistics technician, for a small pharmaceutical firm. The FDA requires a ton of data to get a new drug approved. We work some weird hours sometimes, so I get an afternoon off once in a while."

"Good. And..." pointing at my left hand, "...you're married."

"Yeah, almost two years now. Claire—my wife—is a nurse. She works at Duke Hospital."

"And she's beautiful, right? Ballplayers always seem to have good-looking wives."

"Well, *I* do, anyway. Speaking of which," I glanced at my watch, "I promised Claire I'd pick her up at five, and it's four-thirty now, so I'd better be going." *Another lie, of course, but I have to get out of here.* "Can I get you another drink?"

"No, two is my limit. Nice meeting you, Jake."

"Yeah, me too."

I went back to the bar, where Sam was obviously poised for news about me and Honey. "Put all that on my tab, Sam. I'm going home."

"Alone?" he said, glancing back at the booth.

"Yes, Sam. Alone!" I barked. "And be sure you get her out of here before the raunchy crowd shows up."

"Raunchy? My customers aren't…"

"Do it, Sam! Her name is Barbara Kelly, and…well, she'll explain."

I went out the back door, hopped into my car, drove to the far end of the parking lot, opened my door and sat on the edge of the seat. I didn't want Barbara to see me when she came out of Sam's, and I didn't want to barf on Sam's section of the parking lot. I opened my wallet and took out my time-worn copy of the same news clipping Barbara had shown me. *Damn! Damn! Damn! I should never have come back to Durham. And how will I ever explain all this to Claire?*

* * *

The next few days were hellish. I was irritable at work and probably would have been at home, too, but Claire was working the swing shift and I didn't see her much. The Bulls were in town, so I went to every game and sat in the bleachers to drink beer and think. Nothing magic happened. I worked Saturday and was moody on Sunday. After I had snapped "Yes, yes" to Claire's "Are you OK?" a couple times, she let me be.

I worked late Monday and took off Tuesday afternoon , but to avoid facing Barbara, I didn't go to Sam's. Claire was back on days that week, so when she came home she found me watching ESPN with the sound muted.

"You didn't go to Sam's?"

"No"

"And you're drinking scotch." She plopped down in a chair facing me. "OK, Jake. You've been grouchy for a week. What's going on?"

"Long story. Ugly. You won't like it."

"Try me. In my job I hear a lot of ugly stories."

I told her about Barbara and showed her the newspaper clipping.

"Oh, that's just awful," she said. "Can you help her?"

"Yes, but that's where it gets…dicey."

"Because…?"

"Because I know what happened that night, and it was…it was my fault."

"*Your* fault. Why?"

"Well, I was with Ted Kelly when he called Barbara that Labor Day in 1999. There were six or seven of us players who had drinks and supper together after the game. The rest of them left to pack up and head for home, but Ted and I were still celebrating. I overdid it: too many drinks, too many pills. Ted was OK, though. Always was. We finally left the restaurant about ten-thirty. Ted had this old British Morgan right-hand-drive sports car that I'd always wanted to drive. He shouldn't have let me, of course, but he was so excited about being called up to Tampa that I talked him into it. I took us out onto highway 98 and we were doing fine—not too fast, even—until we met that truck. It came up suddenly over a rise and I...I just didn't react fast enough. The truck *was* in our lane, and I swerved to avoid it, but too late. Ted was in the passenger seat, so he took the worst of the crash. Somehow I was thrown clear and woke up in the ditch. The Morgan was totaled and Ted was in it, dead. The truck was on its side in the middle of the road and the driver was dead, too."

Claire was crying, and clutched my hand. I downed the rest of my scotch. She sniffled and said, "Go on, Jake."

"Well, I panicked. I was twenty-eight years old and a few days away from the last chance I'd ever have to play big-league baseball. I couldn't risk being involved in an auto accident where two people died. No other cars had come by, so I pulled Ted's body into the driver's seat and hooked the seat belt. Then I walked back towards town. I had a badly sprained knee and maybe a broken collarbone, so it was painful, but I had to get away from there. If I saw a car coming, I'd duck into the ditch or the woods. After what seemed like forever I found an all-night convenience store and called a cab. I'd been sharing an apartment with two other players that year, but they both moved out right after the game. Ted was living alone that summer because Barbara had spent a lot of time with him. So no one was expecting either of us back that night. I stayed inside a couple days and patched myself up, like ballplayers often do when they want to keep playing. The Rays did call me up, and I played in six or seven games over the next two weeks. Batted about .150 and made four throwing errors. They released me at the end of the season."

Claire had stopped crying and now just looked puzzled. "Jake, I just don't understand why..."

"I'm coming to that. My baseball career was over, but I was still scared that I'd get blamed for the accident, so I moved to the west coast. An old buddy in San Jose gave me a job in his sporting goods store, but I was still popping pills and got busted. The judge sent me to drug rehab, which turned out to be a 'blessing in disguise.' This was 2000 and some minister at the rehab house told us to 'Make a new life in the new millennium.' Hokey, I know, but it gave me an idea. I changed my name from Joseph Alberto Francona to Jacob Alan Fowler. Same initials, I know. I guess people often do that. I enrolled at a community college and got a two-year degree in statistics, which must be second nature to baseball players, like being superstitious, because I liked it. That led to a job at Grenoble Pharmaceuticals in Santa Clara, and then in 2004 Grenoble merged with another company here in Durham and I was relocated. The idea of coming back here scared me at first, but five years had passed and I figured that anyone I knew here had probably moved away. And I had changed my appearance, too. Put on some weight, grown this beard and starting wearing glasses. I was right, I guess, because Barbara didn't recognize me. Does that answer your question?"

"Well maybe and maybe not," she said angrily, then stood up and screamed at me. "Dammit, Jake—or whoever you are—how could you do this to me? I'm your wife! I've got two years of my life invested in you, and I was planning on a whole lot more. I botched one marriage because I—well, both of us—were too independent and too secretive. I'm not going to let that happen again. You've got to talk to me, Jake. No matter what it's about. And right away, not two years later."

"I just didn't..."

"I know. But we have to trust each other, or it'll never work."

"OK. I'll try to do better."

"I damn sure hope so!" She took a deep breath, stared hard at me and sat down again. "I feel terribly sorry for Barbara, but what happened to her brother wasn't your fault."

"Maybe it was, Claire. That's something I'll never know."

"Well, *I* know," she said. "I know you."

"You know Jake Fowler. You didn't know Joe Francona. Different guy."

"Well, maybe. But some things don't change."

We both just sat there, quiet for a while. Then Claire said, "You have to tell her, Jake. Tell Barbara what really happened."

"I just can't." I swallowed hard. "Not because of I'm still scared for myself, but Ted was a rookie, six years younger than me, and my friend. I should have looked out for him, and I didn't."

"We have to find a way to help her, though...some roundabout way...through Sam, maybe?"

"No. I like Sam, but he's not much on keeping secrets. That's why he has three ex-wives."

"But...how about her attorney? She must have one here that's working on her case."

"Yeah. Good idea. I'll find out who he is."

"There's one other thing I need to know, Jake."

"Yeah?"

"When you changed your name, it was all legal, right?"

"Yeah."

"So we are really married?"

"Yes, dear."

"OK, then, you don't have to sleep on the couch tonight."

✳ ✳ ✳

I called Barbara the next morning.

"Hi, Jake. I missed you at Sam's yesterday."

"Yeah, had to work. You had any luck finding old ballplayers?"

"Well, Sam pulled in a few for me, but none of them knew Ted very well. I'm still hopeful, though. You got anything for me?"

"No, but how about giving me your attorney's name and number, just in case I find someone and you're not in town."

"Sure," she said, and gave me the information.

The next morning I walked into the offices of Yarbrough & Holman in the old CCB building downtown.

"Do you have an appointment, Mr. Fowler?" the receptionist

inquired.

"No, but tell Mr. Yarbrough that I have some important information on the Ted Kelly case."

Before long I was seated across a conference table from a well-groomed, fiftyish, black man wearing rimless glasses and a skeptical expression. On the table was a bulky, dog-eared file with *T. KELLY—9925* on the spine, a yellow legal pad and a small tape recorder.

"I'm Donald Yarbrough," he said. "What's your interest in this matter, Mr. Fowler?"

"I met Barbara Kelly recently and she told me about some of the problems you're having with this case."

"And…"

"Well, I can tell you exactly what happened the night Ted Kelly died because…because I was there."

"Do you mind if I record our conversation, Mr. Fowler?"

"No, not at all. And call me Jake."

"OK, Jake. Folks call me Donald. Go ahead."

I told him the whole story, just as I had told it to Claire. He listened and made some notes. He interrupted once to get the names of the other players who had been with Ted and me at supper that night. When I finished he turned off the recorder.

"An intriguing story, Jake. Would you swear to it in court?"

"Yes. It's all true."

"What about these two witnesses TriState has who say Ted was drunk or high that night?"

"Well, they're wrong. Who are they, Donald, do you know?"

He pulled a sheet from his file. "Carl Cooper, a Bulls player, and Bruce Lippman, one of the trainers."

"Wow. Cool Carl and Bruiser. A real pair of losers. Listen, Donald, Cooper was a mediocre outfielder who had a gambling problem and was always bumming money from the rest of us. He'd say anything for a fifty-buck loan. And Bruiser was making more money off unofficial steroid shots than from his salary."

"Unreliable sources, you would say." Yarbrough was grinning.

"Yes, and anyone from that '99 team would agree with me."

"Good." He leaned forward. "At this point I should remind you that I am not your attorney and therefore this conversation is not privileged. If you *did* give this evidence in court, you would be admitting to some serious crimes, such as leaving the scene of an accident, obstructing justice and perhaps even vehicular homicide. You could go to prison for several years. Do you understand that?"

"Yes," I gulped. "I'll take that risk. I'm really more concerned that then Barbara would know about me. Can we avoid that?"

"Hmm. Well, I can't guarantee that, but I'll do my best. Let me get your statement typed up and have you sign it. I believe I can use it as leverage to push Tri-State into a fair settlement without going to trial. They don't really want to go to court on this, anyway, because my client would get a lot of sympathy from a jury. Thank you, Jake. You've been very helpful."

When I told Claire about my visit with Yarbrough, she said, "He sounds like a good man. Do you trust him?"

"Yes."

"So I shouldn't worry about you going to prison or anything nasty like that?"

"No, you shouldn't." *She will, of course, and I will, too. But it has to be this way now or I'll never feel right about it.*

* * *

For what seemed like forever I didn't go to Sam's and didn't hear from Barbara. Then Yarbrough called.

"I've been talking with Tri-State's attorney, Jake. Your affidavit hit them pretty hard, though he won't admit it. He's asked to meet with you. He probably wants to decide how credible you'd be on the witness stand. You don't have to do it. But if you're willing, we can do it here in my office, where you might be more comfortable."

"Donald, I was always a little intimidated by left-handers throwing high fastballs, but some guy shuffling papers doesn't scare me. Set it up."

* * *

Harvey Cantrell probably does intimidate some people. He's about six-three, distinguished-looking and speaks with assurance. We all chatted pleasantly about baseball and families for a while, then Cantrell got down to business.

"You tell a good *story*, Mr. Fowler," he said, tossing my affidavit onto the table. "Why should anyone believe it?"

"Because it's true, I suppose," I replied with a smile.

"I have two witnesses who say otherwise."

"Yeah, so I heard. Cooper and Lippman. One's probably being hunted by those guys who enforce gambling debts and the other is likely wanted by the vice squad. They'll both say anything to make a deal and save their own skins. I can find ten other guys—good guys—who will say that Ted Kelly never drank more than two beers or popped a pill." *I wasn't sure I could actually do that, but it seemed like a good bluff, and he apparently bought it.*

"All right, Mr. Fowler. Let's say, hypothetically, that we believe your version of what happened that night—something you apparently failed to mention to anyone for almost nine years. You were driving the car, and you *were* drunk, by your own admission, so…"

"Yes, I was driving, and I had been drinking earlier in the evening, but was I drunk? Nobody knows, and it's a little late now for a breathalyzer test. But regardless of all that, your client's truck *was* on the wrong side of the road and hit us almost head-on."

"Well, you say so, but nobody knows that, either, so…"

Donald cut him off. "The police do, Leo. After hearing Jake's story, I re-read the final accident reports. They found skid marks in the eastbound lane where Jake swerved to avoid the truck, but no skid marks at all for the truck. Your driver never tried to avoid the collision."

Cantrell pursed his lips and frowned, probably pretending to ponder the situation. Turning to Yarbrough, he said, "Well then, perhaps we should consider a settlement. This case has dragged out much too long and I'm sure your client—and you, too, of course—would like to see some cash. As I recall, the last offer we made was $800,000, which your client refused. I believe I could get my client to increase that offer to one million. Would that be satisfactory?"

"I think not," said Yarbrough smoothly. "We had asked for $1.5 million, and before Tri-State came into the picture I think Lighthouse was ready to give us $1.2 million. In view of the additional evidence we now have, I don't see how I could now recommend that my client accept even that amount."

"Donald, I'm sure you appreciate that I have to show my client some, ah, progress for all the time and effort I've put into this matter. *And*," looking back to me, "I'm sure that Mr. Fowler, nee Francona, would prefer that his affidavit not become available to the Durham County DA's office."

"Don't try to blackmail me, Cantrell," I said. "At this point, I don't care."

"OK then. Donald, I think you should take my offer to your client and let *her* decide. Gentlemen, I think that concludes our meeting. Good day." Cantrell gathered his papers and left.

"You did great, Jake. He won't risk going to court now. I'll talk to Barbara…"

"But no concessions just for my sake, Donald. I mean it!"

"OK, OK. I still have some negotiating to do, though. I'll keep you posted."

* * *

When I told Claire about the meeting, she said, "That sounds good for Barbara, but…would Cantrell really do that, Jake? Give your testimony to the DA just out of spite?"

"No, I don't think so. Don't worry about it." *But she probably did, and so did I.*

Fortunately, not for long. About three weeks later, Donald called.

"The deal is done, Jake, and you're in the clear. Thanks again for…"

"How much?"

"I can't discuss the details.'

"And Barbara doesn't…"

"I can't discuss the details. Attorney-client privilege and all that stuff."

"Well, OK then. Great job, Donald. I enjoyed working with you."

"Me, too, Jake. Maybe we'll see each other again sometime. Bye, now."

I gave the news to my anxious-looking Claire, who threw her arms around my neck and cried. "I'm so happy for you. And for Barbara, too. Do you think she knows it was you who helped her?"

"I have no idea. Donald wouldn't tell me."

"I don't suppose I'll ever have a chance to meet her, will I?"

"As much as I would like that, I think it's better that you don't. Better for me, that is."

* * *

On the Tuesday after Labor Day, I went back to Sam's for the first time in almost four months.

"Hey there, Jake. Long time no see. You been OK?" Sam quickly placed a cold Michelob in front of me.

"Yeah, fine. Just real busy."

We talked for a while about likely World Series teams and local politics. Then Sam said, "Say, you remember Barbara, that cute honey-blonde you talked with here one night?"

"Sure. Nice kid. Why you ask?"

"Well, look at this." He handed me the sports section of the *Raleigh News & Observer*. On the first page was a picture of Barbara, flanked by the Mayor of Durham, the Bulls' manager and a middle-aged couple, all standing at home plate and smiling, with the Labor Day crowd in the background. The story below said:

FORMER PLAYER'S MEMORIAL TO BENEFIT LOCAL YOUTH

Ted Kelly went 15-2 for the Bulls in 1999, his first year of pro baseball, and was slated to finish that season with the Tampa Devil Rays. But he died that Labor Day when a delivery truck demolished his small car on Highway 98 east of Durham.

At the Bulls' game yesterday, Kelly's sister Barbara announced the creation of the Ted Kelly Memorial Foundation, which will support baseball and other programs for underprivileged youth in Durham. The Foundation is endowed with the proceeds of the Kelly family's wrongful death suit against the delivery truck's company, just recently settled. The

Kellys declined to disclose the amount of the settlement, but rumor has it well in excess of $1 million.

Barbara Kelly expressed gratitude to her attorney, Donald Yarbrough, for "sticking with us for almost ten years without getting paid" and to an unnamed witness who provided crucial information to overcome the contention that Ted Kelly himself had caused the fatal collision.

"Gee, that's great," I said.

"Yeah, sure is. You ever see her again after that one time?"

"No, but I'm glad things worked out so well for her."

I stayed at Sam's that afternoon, and it felt good. On the way home I picked up the N&O and cut out the picture and story Sam had shown me. When I got home I put that clipping in the back of my dresser drawer. Then I took the old 1999 clipping out of my wallet, crumpled it and threw it in the wastebasket. That felt good, too.

About the author:

Herb Wakeford is a semi-retired CPA who has lived in Raleigh, North Carolina since 1970. He has always enjoyed writing, but his earlier efforts were found mostly in business publications. Herb is now writing short stories, poetry, humor and mysteries. He also teaches tax courses for the OLLI/Encore program at NC State University and participates in Encore's Writers Group. He is a native of Minneapolis and an honors graduate of the University of Minnesota. Herb and his wife Molly have four children and seven grandchildren, none of whom are accountants.

THE DAY BETWEEN SUNDAY AND MONDAY
©2015 by Ronna L. Edelstein

She feels like Norman Bates's mother, slumped in a rocking chair, not quite alive, but not quite dead. Vera's descent into the symbolic basement of her life began more than two years ago when an ache in her mouth turned into a debilitating pain that required two surgeries: removing the disk in her left jaw joint and later replacing that disk with one made from her own tissue and held in place with three screws. Tomorrow—she chose a Monday because "back-to-work miserable Monday" seems the perfect setting for her possible demise—she faces her third and most complex surgery—a total jaw replacement. Vera is scared, but living a life of "cannots" scares her even more.

She cannot use an adult-sized toothbrush or have dental x-rays because she can barely open her mouth. She cannot chew a steak, munch on her favorite red licorice, or eat a toasted bagel. She can only devour her beloved M&Ms—sugar-filled pellets of cholesterol—because the candy lives up to its "melt in your mouth" promise. Vera cannot enjoy theatre because the sword fights in her jaw and joint distract her from the drama on stage. She cannot laugh at comedies because using her "happy muscles" creates electric shocks in her head. Vera cannot walk the treadmill, something she has done for thirty years since she turned thirty, because her feet pounding against the moving belt jolts her with pain. She cannot socialize at night because she is too tired from all the sleepless nights of pain. She cannot put on make-up because even the contact between the fine bristles of the brush and her cheek hurts.

Most of all, Vera cannot imagine a life as a dead person. When the topic of death overwhelms her, as it frequently does since she lives with her 91-year-old father and best friend, she reverts to her usual way of handling the subject: humor. Vera starts every day by reading the obituaries. Not finding her name, she knows she is good to go for at least another twenty-four hours.

She wishes she had a stronger foundation than black comedy to deal with the inevitable. Yet, faith is believing in something without evidence to support that belief. And Vera is a "prove it to me" person. At one point, a few months after Ma died several years earlier, Vera almost thought she had the empirical data she needed to have faith in the afterlife when she discovered 1) a strand of red thread lying atop a white t-shirt; Ma always sewed with red thread; 2) a five-dollar bill on the sidewalk; Ma always sent the grandchildren notes with a five-dollar bill enclosed; and 3) a bobby pin lying on the floor; Ma always used bobby pins to keep stray hairs in place. She was convinced that these findings were signs of Ma communicating and telling her to believe she was okay and that there was a kind of life after death. Then, she heard nothing more, and Vera's faith weakened.

As Vera lies in bed the Sunday-before-the-Monday, she wishes someone would come back after being gone for a few days or, better yet, a few weeks, and hold a lecture on What Lies Beyond. She would need definite proof that this person had really died, spent time in some kind of refrigeration, and was not just hallucinating about a near-death experience.

Then, Vera hears a knocking on her door, taps that imitate the drumming of the theme song of the old *Dragnet* television series. It is Dad's way of checking, "Is it okay for me to come in?" And it is. He arrives with a tray sitting in the basket of his walker. The tray contains one bowl of cereal—Vera's special combo of rounded oats and leaf-like flakes—a spoon small enough for her uncooperative jaw, and a medium-sized glass of milk, a liquid the same blue as the veins the anesthetist will puncture in less than 24 hours. Dad responds to Vera's startled look by smiling and, in a Dr. Seuss imitation, saying, "This is your day. Eat your breakfast and let's be on our way."

And so Dad leads Vera on a magical day where the dark thoughts of anesthesia and needles and ghoul-like physicians fade, replaced by the joy of Father/Daughter time.

With his wheelchair in the trunk and walker in the backseat, Dad directs Vera to drive the scenic route from their apartment to the glass building that always reminds Vera of an old-fashioned orange juice squeezer. The building is the city's showcase for flora and fauna—and the setting where Dad and Vera lose themselves for the next ninety minutes.

Vera has never had a box of crayons that could capture the nuanced colors of each room of the building. Just as she gushes to Dad, "This room is the best," they enter another area that surpasses the one they have just left. From his wheelchair, Dad tries to teach Vera the scientific names of the different flowers and plants, but she likes giving them fantasy names: the umbrella plants—those tree-like plants whose green leaves will protect her even from the huffing and puffing of the wolf in "The Three Little Pigs"—or from the cutting of the surgeon's scalpel; the Peter Cottontail plants—those fluffy red balls that remind her of the puffs Grandma used to apply her powder and rouge; the ballerina plants—those blue flowers that seem to gracefully sway and move when kissed by even a breath of air. All of the freshly watered flowers and plants shine like stars against a grassy green sky.

As Vera and Dad explore every corner and pathway of the exhibit, they talk about how the two of them, from the time Vera turned seven until she became a teenager, had always gone to the annual Flower Show in this very building. This yearly Sunday event was only for Father and Daughter; no mother, brother, or grandmother was allowed. Before leaving the house, Ma would take a picture of Vera and Dad with the family's Brownie camera; each new photo replaced the one from the previous year in the silver-plated frame that still stands on Vera's dresser and still holds a favorite Father/Daughter picture. Dad always wore a gray suit with a matching gray hat, sensible black shoes, and the necktie Vera had given him for his birthday the month before. Vera always thought he looked regal—a dashing Prince Charming.

Vera had also dressed in her best outfit. Like Dad, she had worn a suit—either bubblegum pink or a soft shade of blue, her two favorite colors. Her patent leather shoes had sparkled like the Hall of Mirrors she and her daughter would visit decades later at Versailles. Vera had accessorized her outfit with white cotton gloves with lace at the wrists and white cotton socks with ruffles at the ankles.

Today, on the Sunday before the "what if" Monday, Dad and Vera reminisce about the Flower Shows of yesteryear. Vera tells Dad that taking her to these shows made her feel like a princess in her own Eden—a garden safe from slithering serpents like the neighbor who would not let her walk on her part of the sidewalk or the classmates who teased her about her tall height. She reminds Dad of the delicious dinner of roast, potatoes, vegetables, and homemade apple pie that Grandma had prepared ahead of time and that awaited them at Grandma's apartment.

Dad leans back in his wheelchair and listens as Vera recalls these special times together. Vera notices tears in his eyes; she wonders whether he cries for Grandma—his mother—who has been gone for decades, for the way time has debilitated him, or for the surgery that casts a shadow even on this magical day. She imagines his tears are for all these reasons.

With the aroma of the flowers following them, Vera and Dad leave the building and travel the short distance to the library. In planning the perfect day, Dad had discovered that the library had scheduled a writer to speak about her books and the writing process. He knows this lecture will be the ideal one for Vera, a woman who has a poster of Shakespeare hanging above her desk and considers any published author a superhero, and he is right. Vera loses herself in the dusty but comforting scent of the books, the cadence of the Irish speaker's words, and the love for language that emanates from the speaker. Just being in the library gives Vera a sense of peace, for one of her earliest memories involves Dad taking her for a hot dog and chili dinner at the diner across from the old library and then up the stone steps into the marble foyer of the library itself. With Dad, she had travelled *East of the Sun and West of the Moon*, lived in a *Little House on the Prairie*, and solved mysteries with Nancy Drew. With Dad, she had gone to Imagi-Nation, a place where no one would ever whisper behind her back, betray her for a more popular girl, or laugh when Vera, a gangly twelve-year-old, still could not do the forward roll in gym class. Thanks to Dad, Vera had lifelong friends in books; those stories, which comforted her throughout the years, would help her get through the surgery of Monday.

After the lecture, Vera wheels Dad to the poetry section. The two read Rudyard Kipling's "If," the poem Dad had encouraged Vera to memorize as a fifteen-year-old, the same age he had been when he had learned the poem. Dad taught Vera to "keep her head when all about her were losing theirs," that cud-chewing cows always look more sensible than gum-chewing girls, and that a cup of hot Ovaltine in the winter or a glass of a bubbling chocolate phosphate in the summer could soothe the sting of a boy's rejection at a dance, a teacher's criticism of awkward attempts to write in cursive, and a mother's dismissal at being too fat or too awkward or too shy.

Thanks to Dad, Vera became a voracious reader. Yet, she has never come across a book that explains how her father, the man who never called anyone "Dad," succeeded in becoming the perfect father, grandfather, and great grandfather. She has never read one author who can help her strip away the layers to discover that inner something that makes Dad so special—and that results in his giving her this special day.

Across from the library is a park. For several years, Dad and Vera have called this park their "staycation" destination—the place they go to in order to relax, reflect, and read. Dad knows that on this particular Sunday, Vera needs to step off the fast-moving treadmill of her daily life and unwind in this urban paradise. She needs to think of something other than her pain by feeding the birds, marveling at how the smaller ones push the larger pigeons out of the way for a soft crumb or piece of crust. Like the flowers at the exhibit, Vera does not know the names of the flowers in the park, but she does like seeing the red ones with large green leaves sway in the breeze like exotic dancers.

Children, their eyes aglow with excitement, pull their parents to the carousel. They remind Vera of her younger self, rushing into the community amusement park with Dad to celebrate her school picnic.

As always, Dad shares memories with Vera. The vanilla ice cream dripping from Vera's cone onto her shirt reminds him of that wintery day decades earlier when he and she had awakened to a snow globe world. It looked as if all the pixies had sprinkled their magical white fairy dust over the neighborhood. As a three-year-old, Vera had not worried about fathers struggling to put chains on car wheels in order to get to work or mothers digging through mounds of snow to find the glass bottles on the back porch the milkman had hopefully deposited. She did not have concerns for the mailman who would have to trudge through high drifts in order to deliver catalogues and bills. And she did not roar with happiness that school would be closed because she was still young enough to want to go to school in order to be like her older brother.

Dad reminds Vera that all she had thought about on that snow globe day was snow angels and snowballs and snow forts and snowmen and snow fun! After making sure Vera had eaten a healthy oatmeal breakfast, Dad had helped her don her shirt, sweater, jacket, leggings, pants, socks, hat, scarf, gloves, and boots. Holding Dad's hand, Vera had waddled outside to let the day begin. She and Dad had built a snow woman, with Grandma contributing her old summer straw hat for their frosty lady's head and shiny black buttons from her jar of special buttons for the eyes. Ma had warmed Dad and Vera with their first of several cups of hot Ovaltine and marshmallows.

With their snow woman watching over them, Dad and Vera had pulled the wooden sled with silver blades—not as grand as Cinderella's carriage but good enough for Vera—to the top of the street. From that perspective, and with the sun smiling down through the falling snow, the street looked like a white highway paved with diamonds. Spring afternoons of racing across the warm cement to play hide 'n seek with neighbors, summer evenings of lining up to buy treats from the ice cream truck, and fall mornings of browsing through the Book Mobile for a new picture book were forgotten as, with a *whoosh* and a "Wow!" and a "Whee!" Vera and Dad flew down the sloped road. Dad, always gallant, pulled both the sled and her back to the top.

Another cup of hot Ovaltine with marshmallows, this time accompanied with grilled cheese sandwiches, led to the highlight of the day—the aria in an already mesmerizing opera, the climax in a hypnotic mystery replete with tantalizing red herrings, the frog-turns-to-prince scene in a fairy tale. With Vera's help (more verbal encouragement than actual physical labor), Dad built an igloo of snow. The igloo lacked the intricate architecture of the previous summer's sandcastle Dad and Vera had constructed at the beach, but it still radiated a beauty of its own: smooth-as-glass walls, a round roof, and a soft floor, thanks to the old quilt from the basement storage trunk. The igloo was the perfect size for Dad and Vera to sit next to each other—a father and daughter finding comfort in a welcoming shelter and in each other's company. Dad, a lifelong storyteller, entertained her with tales of other blizzards that began with "once upon a time," included daring feats of charming princes and the undying love of beautiful princesses—all named Vera—and ended with "happily ever after." He even taught her the nose-to-nose Eskimo kiss!

Since that storm almost six decades earlier, Vera has experienced many more storms—some caused by nature and some created by human acts committed by others and herself. Yet, as Dad reminds her today in the park, she has managed to survive every natural and emotional tempest in her life. Just as he was by her side then, so will he be with her tomorrow when the aide wheels her into surgery. And he will be with her for the "happily ever after" when she awakens in recovery.

Vera and Dad end the day with a drive through the back roads to the small city where Dad had grown up. After his father died when Dad was only a toddler, Dad and Grandma had moved into the family house. There, grandparents, uncles, and an aunt had indoctrinated Dad with the necessity of being seen, not heard. When Dad turned ten, his mother had remarried a man from a Dickens' novel—an alcoholic who cared little about his biological son, let alone his stepson. Still, this child without a father figure grew into the man who applauded Vera as she rode a pony at the children's zoo, took her on "walks and talks" on brisk spring and autumn days, and even arranged his Monday office schedule so he could take her on a weekly trip to the Five 'n Ten to buy her an outfit for her doll.

The Father and Daughter watch through the car windows as the sun sets, reluctantly yielding its domination of the sky to the moon and its family of stars. A few clouds flirt with the fading sun but, for the most part, the sky is an unblemished blue lit with rays of yellow, orange, and red. It seems as if even Mother Nature understands that this day is unique, that it is not the usual frantic "get-all-the-errands-done Sunday before embarking upon the hectic back-to-work Monday." Instead, it is a special day of sharing and remembering.

Later, Vera lies in bed, unburdened by images of Norman Bates's mother slumped in her rocking chair coffin. She feels the pain emanating from her jaw, but she finds the strength to focus on her day with Dad, not on the electrical-like currents shooting through her skull. Dad's snores penetrate the thin walls of the apartment, lulling Vera with their soothing rhythm. As she falls asleep, she wraps herself in her quilt—and in mentally reliving the day between Sunday and Monday.

About the author:

I am a teacher and a lifelong student, a daughter and a parent, a caregiver to my 98-year-old father and a recipient of others' care. I am a dreamer and a doer, an optimist and a realist, a lover of M&Ms and daily workouts on the elliptical. I am a thinker and a writer.

As a part-time faculty member of the University of Pittsburgh's

English Department, I work as a consultant at the school's Writing Center. I also teach Freshman Programs, a course that introduces students to the University and the city. My work, both fiction and nonfiction, has appeared in *DreamquestOne* (online—first place); *It's All Talk*: Newsletter of the Osher Lifelong Learning Institute at Carnegie Mellon 2013 (book review); New Slang" A New Literary Voice by the Women and Girls of Pittsburgh" (online); *Quality Women's Fiction*; *Ghoti Online Literary Magazine*; *First Line Anthology*; *Take the Path* (Scribes Valley Publishing—first place fiction "Wednesday Night Girl"); *When We Are* (Scribes Valley Publishing—second place fiction "The Visit"); *Visiting Elsewhere* (Scribes Valley Publishing – third place fiction "Push 'n Shove"); *Welcome to Elsewhere* (Scribes Valley Publishing – second place fiction "Snow Woman"); *The Road to Elsewhere* (Scribes Valley Publishing – third place fiction "Ma Bates"); *The Reading Place* (Scribes Valley Publishing—finalist fiction "Dismissed"); *SLAB: Sound and Literary Artbook*; *Pulse: Voices from the Heart of Medicine* (online and print); *AARP Bulletin* (online and print); *Healthy Roots* (Forbes Health Foundation and Hospice); *The Jet Fuel Review* (Lewis University's online literary journal); *Writer's Relief* (online); *Chicken Soup for the Teenage Soul* (1997); and the *Pittsburgh Post-Gazette*.

A SON'S LOVE
©2015 by John Bauer

He that spareth the rod hateth his son: but he that loveth him correcteth him betimes. Withhold not correction from a child: for if thou strike him with the rod, he shall not die. Thou shalt beat him with the rod, and deliver his soul from hell.
--Proverbs 13:24

The two-blade ceiling fan slowly turned above the table, tired like the room's early morning occupants. Two a.m. The deputies and volunteers had worked under a full moon until soft white clouds blanketed her face. They'd been unearthing bodies since midnight. They'd found three headless ones. Morley had said that's all they'd find. Shallow graves. He'd said he'd gotten tired shoveling, too.

"I don't think I'll need a lawyer," Morley began. "Thanks for askin'. Wouldn't mind havin' somethin' to drink, I'm parched." Beads of sweat covered his face and hairy forearms.

"We'll need you to waive your right to counsel on tape," Sheriff T.B. Lester said. He motioned for one of his deputies to fix Morley some tea.

"Even if I'd a thunk I'd done somethin' wrong, I wouldn't hire me an attorney. They all just pigs without lipstick." Nobody laughed. "'Sides, ignorance of the law is on my side." Again no one saw any humor in the situation. Morley started to fidget on the metal bench his bottom completely covered.

"Something wrong before you start?" the Sheriff asked.

"Need to use your facilities," Morley said, grimacing, "Numbah two. Sorry."

"I don't think he'll fit inside the jail stalls, Sheriff," Deputy Smith said. "'Sides, he'd plug up the plumbing and you know our maintenance budget is tight."

"Take him around back and have him use one of those construction Port-a-Johns. Give him a flashlight. Stay with him, Deputy."

"Right, Sheriff," Smith answered, lumbering Morley out of the interrogation room. They returned after a half hour, more or less. Morley re-seated himself and put his hands, palms down, on the table, facing Sheriff Lester. He didn't look him straight in the eye. Instead he looked down and turned his head behind himself every so often, like he thought someone was sneaking up behind him, looking to smack him or do him some harm. This was a nervous habit Morley had developed as a teen.

"I don't have a college education. I haven't been taught the finer points of carin' for and buryin' one's kin. Always done tried my best for Pappy, Momma, and sisters, too. We were a close family, very close, and up until this past week, we always ate supper together." Morley paused and asked, "Can I get a recordin' of what I say, and listen in to it?"

"Sure," Sheriff Lester answered. He wondered whether Morley was literate. He let his question pass.

"I hadn't checked on Pappy right away after I'd arrived back home. I'd first fixed me some fried chicken, mashed taters with gravy, butter beans, sweet corn, corn bread, and some sweet tea to wash it all down. A body's got to eat. Pappy and the others always enjoyed my cookin'. If he was here this minute, he'd tell you my fried chicken was the best in Robbins County. He would've eaten at least two helpin's. I take that back. Since he hadn't eaten all day, he would've been starved. He would've had more than two. No telling how many more, but more than two.

"I hadn't left him *that* long. I'd gone fishin' down by the creek. Didn't catch anythin' and fell asleep. The skeeters and noseeums woke me up. Pappy and the others never liked fishin'. They liked eatin' and sleepin' though. They'd do that plenty while I cared for 'em. But if I made one mistake?" He paused and looked up at his audience, then continued. "Sheriff, you remember that big leather belt that hung above Pappy's bed?" Sheriff Lester nodded. "I'd felt it more than once. Just a few accidents I'd had when I was younger, which were no ways my fault." Morley looked up and glanced over his shoulder. No one moved. No one had moved.

"Being eldest, I raised everyone. Pappy was a long-distance trucker. Momma 'companied him often when he was on the road, expectin' or not. Never got a red cent for child rearin'. I probably wasn't the best sitter in the world, but you get what you pay for. They paid me nothin'.

"I'd get blamed for every accident. I may have been the eldest, but sister Gertrude—we called her Trudy—was always the largest. When we took trips in the family station wagon when it used to work, she *had* to sit next to the window or she got car sick. A spoiled brat she was. Pappy favored her a lot. I should've had some rights as firstborn. At least that's what they said the Good Book said. But no, I had to sit between her and brother Earl, who was always gassin' up with his window closed. Not at all fair. I should've gotten the window seat once in awhile. Was it my fault Trudy's door became accidently unlocked? Was it my fault when it broke open by itself, and Trudy fell out into the road? I don't think I should have been held responsible for her injuries. We weren't traveling that fast. Why'd I have to get strapped?"

Sheriff Lester did not answer Morley. He looked at him and nodded in empathy, silently encouraging him to continue with his story.

"Was lockin' your sisters in the barn on a Saturday afternoon for a few hours, a crime? Earl, Chubb, and I wanted to play baseball. We were young bucks after all. The girls wanted to play house. There were plenty of empty 'frigerators and freezers, which Pappy kept for I have no idear why. They could climb around in 'em in the dark. How was I s'posed to know they would lock themselves in one? Was I responsible for their every mistake? We boys only played until it got twilight. 'Sides, Trudy started breathin' before the doctor said she'd had any permanent brain damage. I let her have the window seat on the next two family trips without complaint. Still, Pappy whipped me good.

"I inherited my forgetfulness from Pappy. One winter, he left Momma outside a St. Helena, Montana truck stop. He remembered he'd forgotten her after several hours. He said the radio's country music had distracted him. She'd lost three toes to frostbite. Don't know she ever forgave him. But she didn't give him a beating.

"Pappy got a burr in his saddle when I had them play "hold yer breath" in the woods. He'd come home and found brothers and sisters hangin' from a couple of oak trees. I would've cut them down before he showed up. Earl was winnin' if we'd kept on. Agin, they had no permanent physical damage. Just some bruised necks. After that one, I couldn't sit down for a good week." Morley glanced side to side, his head flinching.

Sheriff Lester looked around the room at his deputies and then interrupted Morley, "Mr. Sandwich, would you mind telling us what happened recently, the events leading up to your daddy's death?"

"Where was I before I went off course with the accidents?"

"You came home and…" The Sheriff waited for Morley to finish his sentence.

"I fixed supper, then I knocked on Pappy's door and there was no answer. I couldn't even hear him snorin' as he would when he'd be in a deep, deep sleep. So I opened the door a crack, because if he was sleepin', I didn't want to wake him. He'd get real mean and try to use that strap of his on me. I remember sayin' in this voice, 'Pappy...Pappy, you awake? You want supper?' You hear how I've lowered my voice? That's how I said what I said. Whenever I'd talk to him, I did so real respectful-like."

"I could see he wasn't movin'. He was restin' on his bed with his big brown horse-eyes open, staring straight up at the ceiling fan circling around, like he was counting its revolutions. He was still in his candy-striped pajamas. He always loved those PJs. He didn't sweat as much in them. One hundred percent cotton. I'd bought them years ago from Riverbank's Big Men's Clothing Outlet over in Adkinson. Pappy said if he'd had his wish, he'd just as soon die in those PJs as he would his flannel shirt and undies.

"As I neared his face, I put my ear up to his nose real close. He wasn't snorin' for certain. Didn't take a college graduate to tell he was acting just like Momma and sisters this past week. It's been a week. Accidents. I tell you. Accidents aplenty.

"We didn't have health insurance. We didn't have life insurance to pay for burials. So I sat on the edge of Pappy's bed and started to think what I should do. I hadn't eaten for hours. I was starved. I went back into the kitchen and got my supper, and came back in to Pappy's bedroom, and sat on the edge of his bed, and fixed on eatin' and thinkin'. I had a mind he was playin' possum as a trick or somethin'. Maybe he'd wake up and scare me while my mouth was full of taters. Then I'd spit 'em out and make a mess, and he'd whip me for that. But no, he just kept staring at the fan go round and round. He didn't even twitch when a fly or two landed on his nose and ear. That got me to decidin', 'cause flies had always molested him more than me, I'd say.

"I made up my mind then and there—on my own, I might add— that I would call you, Sheriff. I knew you'd know what to do. I voted for you every time you'd run for office. I hadn't ever called you for Momma and sisters because we lived so far out in the woods. I knew y'all have enough work to do every day to be bothering with po' country folks like us. You've real murders and crimes to tend to."

"Mr. Sandwich, how long was it between the time you entered your daddy's room and then called us?"

"I was fixin' to tell you, Sheriff. I don't know exactly. I don't wear a watch," he said, holding up his arms so the Sheriff could verify there wasn't a band which could fit his wrists.

"Go on," Sheriff Lester said. They'd brought several pitchers of ice cold sweet tea in for Morley. There was no air conditioning in the room. In the August heat and humidity, a sweat puddle was forming underneath Morley as he talked.

"Bless your heart, Sheriff," Morley said, "I was parched." He put both hands around one pitcher and drank out of it like a giant. Then he set it down and started his narration again.

"I figured it'd take your boys some time to get to Pappy's place since they'd have to travel the new access road. Gave me some time to finish a second helping. Didn't have any idear why I was so hungry. I decided on my own your boys might be hungry too, so I fixed us all a pecan pie and put coffee on to brew.

"I sat on the front porch waitin' for your deputies, chewin', and waitin' on the pie to get done. Those two," he said, pointing to Deputy Smith and Deputy Harvell, who were standing next to Sheriff Lester, "can tell you the rest of the story."

"I'll get their statements afterwards. I'd like to hear yours first," Sheriff Lester said.

"I don't think they liked that we had a lot of clutter in the house. We needed to have plenty of canned and dried food on hand because we lived so far from town. We never had enough cabinets and pantry space in the kitchen. Everyone had a healthy appetite. That's why boxes were stacked in the hallways.

"I remember them findin' Pappy. He hadn't moved any, his legs wide apart, layin' in his favorite PJs, and eyes still starin' at the fan. I didn't close his eyes because Pappy didn't like to be touched, even much by Momma. I wanted your boys to find him like I had, so I wouldn't be accused of 'movin' the body', so to speak. Not that I'd done anythin' wrong. I've been very cooperative." Then Morley looked up and blurted out, "Am I being accused of anythin'?"

"Let's finish hearing your statement. We've never had a situation exactly like this before," Sheriff Lester answered.

"Fair enough. More than fair. They were a tad surprised at Pappy's size. They saw Pappy's mattress had broken through his box springs and was on the floor. They discussed movin' him out. They radioed back to you, Sheriff, and the Willard Volunteer Fire Department, to see if anyone was available to help. I think they had good luck. Quite a few men showed up after an hour or so.

"I answered all the deputies' questions while we waited for the others to arrive. I don't think y'all want me to repeat myself agin. I told them about me fishin', sleepin', the skeeters and noseeums, and fixing supper, and waitin' for just the right moment to open Pappy's door. He could be hard sometimes, but I'm not going to speak ill of my most recently deceased closest kin.

"I offered them supper. I felt bad they'd come out to our house so late. I asked would they like some chicken? White or dark meat? I remember sayin' I prefer white meat myself. They said they had a hard time digestin' while dinin' *next to dead bodies.* Well, it was only one dead body—Pappy's—when I'd asked. And we could've eaten on the porch, not in Pappy's room.

"Deputy Smith had problems with Pappy's size. Like it was all my fault. As a God-fearing son, sure I cooked for him. Who was I to argue, certainly not with his "leather discipline" hangin' above his bed.

"In Pappy's house, you had to walk through the livin' room to get to the kitchen. Your deputies saw I hadn't quite cleaned up the week's mess. Momma and two younger sisters lived with us up until recently. Brothers moved away years ago. Don't really know why. I really should call them both. They should know Pappy has passed. They live out-of-state, but I'm sure they'll want to know. Would that count as my one phone call, Sheriff?"

"No, we'll give you more than one call, Mr. Sandwich," Sheriff Smith said. It was past three a.m. The deputies were exhausted, but they were as alert as if they'd just drank a gallon of caffeine. "Since you mentioned the rest of your family, maybe you could explain what happened to them at this point in your statement."

"I was fixin' to do just that. Was a run of bad luck this past week, I tell ya', a run of sorry luck. Monday, Gretchen was cleanin' her gun and it accidentally went off. I done showed her from when she was birthed, don't ever put the barrel in your mouth. Not while it was loaded anyway. Wednesday, Trudy tripped down the stairs and snapped her neck like a chicken bone. I feel partially responsible for her accident 'cause I should've fixed the railin' years ago.

"Momma had blood clots and had had several strokes. She had one vein, looked like the Monongahela. She was the least healthy of us all. I did my best to treat her. I'm no doctor, but we couldn't afford to be carryin' her to the hospital every week. I'd learned somethin' in rat poison thinned a person's blood. Didn't take a college graduate to figure out what I'd do. 'Course, I fed her bite-sized portions. Worked for several years. Worked up 'til Friday. She cut herself and dang if I couldn't stop the bleedin'.

"Let me finish up with Pappy. The volunteers and more deputies had arrived. I'd given them the "okay" to cut an openin' through Pappy's bedroom window. The exterior wall wasn't load-bearin'. 'Sides, they had to get Pappy out of the house, one way or the other. I figured I could patch it up afterwards with plastic sheets and duct tape. They dragged Pappy through the chain-sawed portal out the side. They got their arms underneath him and flopped him down the hill. Could see his head bounce like a rollin' stone. Our house is on high ground. I couldn't help them 'cause I've a bad back. I wanted to, though. I wanted to help in the worse way.

"They took several breaks to catch their breath. One of the volunteers was also a farmer by trade. He'd brought his flatbed trailer which he normally used to haul his tractor around on. They rolled Pappy up its ramp and onto its bed. Then they tied him down with rope and bungee cords, so he wouldn't roll off on the way into town. These men should be rewarded for their efforts in the middle of the night, workin' together like they did. I wish I could've ridden with them.

"I thought that was that. But you showed up, Sheriff, and you know the rest. The pecan pie was done, but you, your deputies, and volunteers didn't want to join me in having a slice or two. You said you were 'on duty.' I was just trying to deal with a terrible loss. I'd just lost my Pappy.

"So's you wanted to go to the back porch and ask me some questions. And we did. I just wanted to eat some pie, then catch some sleep, but I felt it'd be better to cooperate. I didn't want you to waste any more county taxpayer dollars out at our home when there were vicious murderers you need catchin' every day. I done told you all that.

"So I turned the porch light on. Big porch light. Thank God I'd fixed the screenin' or we would've been eaten alive by the bugs. Sittin' on my rockin' chair, I could answer your questions between mouthfuls.

"Then you saw the three stone markers, and the soil looked like it'd been turned. I'm goin' to get my cookin' position back at McDonald's first thing Monday. Then I'm goin' to save me up some money and get some really nice gravestones with names and birth dates and all. Did you know Gretchen and Trudy were both born on Halloween?

"I could've lied and told you they was pets buried out back. I done admitted they were family. I cooperated and gave you permission for the volunteers to dig some."

"For the record, you know we're going to have autopsies performed on what we found," Sheriff Lester interjected.

"I reckon you need to do what you think is your job, Sheriff. You just 'member I voted for you and 'member I told you not to waste the county's tax dollars."

"I'll remember. Please continue so we can finish up."

"Not much more to say you don't already know."

"The district attorney would want to hear your explanation in your own words, not mine."

"Pappy told me to bury 'em. He couldn't, well he physically couldn't, help me any. Last several months, he couldn't get out of bed," Morley said. He stopped to drink more sweet tea. "Had to obey Pappy. Had to. Couldn't get them out of the house in one piece." His voice trailed off. He looked behind him. Then he continued.

"I think everyone was sort of surprised when they started to find body parts. One of 'em came up to where we were sittin' with what was a large foot in his spade. Even though it was soiled, I could identify through the screenin' it was 'ol Trudy. She was the larger of the twins.

"The pile of limbs was growing just outside the screen door. You 'member, Sheriff, those volunteers worked fast. 'Sides, the graves weren't that far from us. I'm glad we're here now. I think back at the house, you and everyone were gettin' the wrong idear about me.

"If feedin' them three squares a day is a crime, well, just what is this country comin' to? We ate and prayed together. I loved Pappy, Momma, and sisters. I cared for 'em, maybe over-cared for 'em. Maybe I spoiled 'em. I wasn't the worst son and brother in the world, maybe not the best, but far from the worst."

"So's why am I here? Look at all I've been sayin',and let me go home to bury Pappy besides the others---after you've put them back where you found them. I hope you let your deputies help me. I don't think the taxpayers of this county need to waste any more of their hard-earned money on payin your salaries by holdin' me here and havin' to feed and keep me."

"We'll have the autopsies verify what you said were their causes of death," Sheriff Lester said, "and turn over what we found to the D.A. He'll decide. You needed to get a permit for a family cemetery. You just can't bury kin in your yard without any written permission."

"Is that all? If I'd only known. My own ignorance of the law. My fault, Sheriff. I'll apply for those permits first thing Monday mornin'. How much will they cost? I've time now to make things legally right. I don't have anyone to feed and care for anymore. " Morley stopped to drink more sweet tea. He was working on his second pitcher. There was a salty pond beneath him. "So may I please go now?" he asked after he'd taken his last gulp and wiped his lips.

"We didn't find their heads. Maybe you could shed some light on what you did with them? Sounded like you had a tragic week. A lot of accidents."

"I'll say. Accidents. When God wants to take you from this earth, He will. You heard how we were close. *Very* close. We ate together, but to tell you the truth—and I was raised to tell the truth—Pappy and Momma favored the girls more than me, though *I was eldest*. Why did they have to have more children? That was their decision. They favored them for sure. Didn't bother me one bit. I still cared for all.

"Pappy *forgot* to use the emergency brake one icy night while asleep on a down slope near Pagosa Springs, Colorado. After his back operation, he couldn't truck any more. Disabled. Momma? Disabled.

Sisters? Disabled. Brothers? One's livin' in Arkansas, the other, Tennessee. Please call them. They'll vouch for me. As the eldest, I quit my McDonald's chef's position to care for all the disabled livin' at home. I was the only one who knew how to cook. Sisters? They only knew how to get locked up in 'frigerators or fall out of station wagons or put their necks in a noose. They never even learned how to boil water.

"Like a good son and brother, I fed everyone who lived under our one roof. Didn't matter how they blamed me out when I was younger. Didn't matter how much Pappy had beaten me. The Lord says to hold no grudges. The Lord says to forgive...and I did.

"With my cookin' and their never stoppin' eatin', they all got so very, very big. Got so none of 'em could walk anywhere very far, anymore. They got so big, they couldn't ride in the wagon beside the window anymore.

"Mr. Sandwich, their heads? Where'd you put their heads?" Sheriff Lester interrupted, slightly raising his voice for the first time.

Morley looked up from the table, directly at Sheriff Lester. Almost like he was in a trance, he said, "After the accidents this past week, *Pappy told me* not to call the authorities because we didn't have the moneys for burials and such. We'd spent all the disability money on food. We had the land in back, though. *I had to listen to Pappy.* A son has to obey his father or else suffer the rod.

"I couldn't get each one outside the house by myself, not in one piece. I couldn't cut through bedroom windows either. Didn't have me a chainsaw. You know what the volunteers had to do to get Pappy out. Well, Pappy and I didn't want to be a burden on anyone. Every day you see on the news how heavy folks cost more for health care, insurance, and such. They blame us for all the world's problems. Not the Sandwich family. We didn't cost the American taxpayers a dime until you came by last evenin'.

"So when each passed on to a heavenly world where human flesh was unimportant, yes, I chopped each one up into pieces I could carry out to the yard. Did it in the livin' room. Didn't have time to clean up the mess 'fore your deputies came. You found every one of 'em. They weren't buried that deep.

"Their heads? You wanted to know 'bout their heads. You'll find them in the wagon, back in the woods. Momma in the front next to where Pappy would've been drivin'. Trudy and Gretchen's? They're by the window seats like they would've wanted.

"Pappy? Like the others, I fed him and fed him and fed him until he couldn't move much except to open his mouth and chew. He got so big, he couldn't lift his arms high enough anymore to reach his strap above his head board.

"That's my 'ficial statement, so help me God."

About the author:

John is new to writing fiction and forever grateful to Scribes Valley for this story's selection. Two other original pieces will be published in 2015. Come November's end, he will again complete a NaNoWriMo "novel." Before this literary life's phase, for five years he had tours in Iraq and Afghanistan as a US Department of State's senior governance advisor. For twenty nine years prior, he served as a county manager, department head, and public servant in North Carolina. Born in Brooklyn, raised on Long Island, schooled at Notre Dame and Syracuse, with significant detours to Mexico City and Little Rock, Arkansas, he is most obviously a senior citizen. He resides in Wilmington, North Carolina, awaiting the welcome baby-sitting duties associated with the birth of his third grandchild in the New Year.

THE JOURNEY
©2015 by Brenda Watterson

Elise finished frosting the cake—red velvet, Nick's favorite. She stood back, licking the last of the chocolate from her fingers and admired her creation. It was perfect. Just like this Father's Day would be. She tried not to think about last year and the separation that almost ripped her family apart. A lot had changed since then; Nick had moved back home and they were working things out. She cleaned up the kitchen and moved the cake to the center of the table. Glancing at her watch, her eyes widened. Shit. It was almost four o'clock. If she didn't leave now she would be late picking up the boys. She grabbed her car keys, but didn't see her shoes.

"Oscar!" she yelled with her hands pressed to her hips.

The lab-shepherd mix they adopted from a shelter six months ago had been described as "curious" and "spirited." She should have seen right through that description. What it really meant was "destructive" and "hyper." Oscar trotted into the kitchen wagging his tail. His nails clicked against the hardwood floor. He looked up at her with liquid brown eyes and her white flip-flop between his teeth. She glared at him, her eyebrows squeezed together and pointed to the shoe. Lowering his head, he dropped his treasure to the ground. Elise picked up the slobbery flip-flop and examined it for damage. Only a few tiny teeth marks lined the heel. She found the mate underneath the dining room table and inspected it too. It looked like she saved them just in time. Ignoring the dog slobber, she slipped them on and headed out the door with a smile. She just knew this was going to be a great summer. She didn't know that by the end of it, she would be dead.

They were just ordinary flip-flops. Foam rubber soles with plastic straps. They had a funny smell like iodine and pesticide, most likely from the packing material they arrived in. They came from a warehouse in Shenzhen, China, an aging factory with no windows or air conditioning. Small Asian workers, many of them children, lined the conveyer belts, paper masks stretched across their faces. The smell of stale sweat and burnt rubber hung in the air. It clung to the walls and permeated their hair and clothing. The factory produced 900,000 pairs of flip-flops that year, including the pair that would eventually find Elise.

Last October, Elise's future flip-flops were individually bagged, boxed and loaded onto a boat headed for the US. They passed through customs and entered the receiving dock in New York, where they were loaded onto pallets. A forklift driver named Lou transferred the delivery to a dark warehouse where starving rats roamed the perimeters. In November, Elise was checking her Thanksgiving turkey when the box holding her future flip-flops were loaded onto the eighteen-wheeler headed to Houston. She finished her Christmas shopping in the same Target store that her flip-flops would eventually arrive. In January, she celebrated her thirty-ninth birthday while her new flip-flops waited patiently in the stockroom, stacked neatly next to plaid shorts from Bangladesh and Polo shirts from Vietnam.

In February, the store pulled their winter clearance to the back. Sandals, swimsuits and tank tops were pushed forward, greeting customers at the door as they stomped fresh snow from their boots.

A middle-aged clerk named Betsy unpacked the box of white flip-flops that held Elise's. Standing in front of a large wall of empty pegs, she tore open the bags and hung each pair by size. For thirty-two days, the pair that would belong to Elise went undisturbed. Spring-breakers leafed through the vast wall of hanging beach shoes, occasionally bumping into Elise's but always grabbing the size above or the color beside them. It was March 21st when her shoes finally found her.

She browsed apparel first, the front wheel of her red cart squeaking in protest as she approached the shoes. The colorful wall of flip-flops reminded her of bare toes and pedicures. Her hand reached for the second peg from the top and her fingers closed around the plastic hanger that held her destiny.

Three months later, at the end of June, she threw the white flip-flops in her suitcase next to her red swimsuit, SPF 30, and wide-brimmed beach hat. Her shoes traveled through the airport without incident. The FTA employee recognized the familiar shape through the security X-ray, but kept his attention on the threat of liquid mouthwash and shampoos. The flip-flops posed no danger.

On the second day of their vacation in the Florida Keys, Elise got up early before the kids. Carefully stepping over pool toys and wet towels from the day before, she peeked into the boy's room and smiled at the tousled blond hair that poked out from each blanket. Nick had rented bikes for the week, and she decided to go for an early ride. She got dressed, threw on Nick's ball cap and grabbed her iPod. She was already downstairs when she remembered her running shoes beside the bed. Not wanting to waste any more of the morning, she glanced around their rented condo until she saw them: her white flip-flops beside the couch. She slid her tanned feet inside them and walked out the door.

The narrow bike path that ran parallel to Rt 24 was packed with joggers and other bikers. Elise rode for ten miles under the morning sun before turning back. Sweat glistened on her forehead and rolled down her neck like teardrops. She was just approaching the crosswalk when her foot slipped forward and fell off the pedal. She pulled back too quickly, lodging the pedal between her flip-flop and bare heel. If she hadn't glanced down to correct her footing, her front tire wouldn't have wavered. Maroon 5 pumped through her headphones, drowning out the screams of the pedestrians that watched the front end of her bike enter the path of the truck.

The driver knew before he hit her that he could not stop in time.

He threw his weight into the brakes anyway, arching his back, and bracing his outstretched arms against the steering wheel. A gold crucifix swung like a pendulum from his rearview mirror as a string of profanities left his lips. The smell of melting rubber filled his nostrils. His tires begged for traction against the asphalt, but it was no use. He closed his eyes as metal and bone collided.

The first EMTs to arrive at the scene were local volunteers. The older of the two men shook his head while the younger man fell to his knees and retched. Traffic was backed up for hours as police questioned witnesses and the local ME confirmed the obvious. A crowd of horrified bystanders stood nearby, pointing and speaking in hushed voices; others stood silent, their fingers stacked horizontally across their mouths as if to stifle silent screams. They watched as her personal effects were collected and dropped into plastic bags; the last being a single white flip-flop. It had been thrown the farthest from her body but lay perfectly intact. It sat waiting in the road, still and silent. It's journey now complete.

About the author:

Brenda Watterson is a former career woman turned SAHM. Now that all four kids are in school she has coaxed her muse out of hiding and unleashed her dream to write. Some recent publications include, "Chicken Soup for the Soul", "Pooled Ink", "Rainbowtreekids.com", "Allparenting.com", "WOW Women on Writing", "Write On" and a piece she wrote about step-parenting that was featured on the "Listen to your Mother" show. She lives in Algonquin, IL with her husband and four children where she writes until the school bell rings.

HOW WILL I LIVE WITHOUT HIM
©2015 by Marlene Olin

For ten years Avery's father had been slowly dying. Murray had been a youthful seventy. He skied in Colorado and rollerbladed on South Beach. Then his warranty ran out. First there was prostate cancer. Then routine surgery on his gall bladder screwed up his pancreas. Before long the once strapping six-foot-two *bon vivant* couldn't even stand up straight. Spinal stenosis on top of everything else.

His third wife was thirty years younger and not the nurturing type. A travel agent, Arlene was looking forward to her retirement. But instead of seeing Tuscany, she was tethered to the Early Bird Special. And Murray wasn't as much fun as he used to be. In fact, after getting home from the office he barely spoke at all.

"He hits the couch and sleeps," she complained to Avery. "Doesn't talk for hours."

On occasion he mustered some energy: Sundays when they went for bagels at the Miramar diner, Thursdays when they ate stone crabs at the Lobster Shack. "He flirts with all the waitresses." Arlene hissed. "You'd think he'd find a word or two for me." Soon he didn't have the energy to flirt.

Arlene had a picture in her head of what a husband should be, and all of a sudden Murray didn't match up. But Avery wasn't surprised. His father never wasted words or showed affection. He'd vegetate for hours on his green La-Z-Boy, propped like a king on his throne. A houseful of kids would cry for his attention. Paper airplanes would sail past his head. But Murray posed like a statue, his clenched marbled hands holding the newspaper, his head buried up to his ears. Murray always sat on the sidelines as if raising two boys was a spectator sport.

Avery's stomach would knot the instant the phone rang. He'd beg his wife, Charlotte, to answer it. "Tell Arlene I'm not home. I'm in the witness protection program. Tell her that I've suddenly died."

Charlotte would put her hands on her hips."Pick up the receiver, Avery." She threw in gestures she saw football coaches practice on TV, pumping her elbows, waving her fists. "You can do this, Avery!" Then she'd shake and shimmy like a college cheerleader until her husband gave in.

As usual, Arlene's voice left him vibrating in pain. "Your father looks right through me. Right through me," she screamed. "Just like I'm a fricking ghost!"

Avery nodded. He knew that look, the look that said you're boring. You're not worth my time.

He was sixteen the day his father sat him down at the kitchen table and poured two tumblers of Johnny Walker. "You need to get laid, Son." He pried open Avery's hand and pressed a wad of condoms into his palm. Avery was the president of his school chess club and had near perfect scores on his SATs. It was ridiculous how little his father knew about his life.

His face reddened. "But I don't have a girlfriend yet, Dad!" He wanted to melt into a puddle on the floor.

"I'm talking about sex, for Christ's sake! Do I need to buy you a goddamned manual?"

Then Avery got the look, the ghost look. Murray's lips snarled, his whole face spelled disappointment. Carrying his drink in one hand and a box of cigarettes in the other, he shuffled back to the TV. "Tim!" he bellowed, calling Avery's brother, reaching for a lifeline. "Where's Tim?"

It occurred to no one—not Arlene, not Avery, not the waitresses and salesclerks who he flirted with—that Murray had Alzheimer's.

He had memorized a script of *how-do-you-dos, you're looking fine, everything's swell*. But one day Arlene found the car keys in the fridge. The next week Murray left the house wearing nothing but his boxer shorts.

"I can't deal with this!" Arlene shouted.

Avery held the phone at arm's length. He looked at it, turned it upside down and sideways, and imagined his fingers crushing his stepmother's head. "What do you want me to do?" asked Avery. "Lojack my father?"

Arlene had made a decision. She had just finished re-upholstering the couch and hanging new drapes. There was no way she was vacating the premises. "I'm putting a fucking stamp on his forehead and shipping him out," she hollered to Avery. "He's your problem now." *Click*.

Avery reluctantly dialed another number. Nothing made him feel lonelier than talking to his brother. But Murray was his problem, too.

"Dad and Arlene are having"—Avery groped for the right phrase—"some issues." He didn't want to say the words. His fears were pulsating like a jellyfish, thrusting themselves forward. Maybe they were all jumping to the wrong conclusion. Murray was the type of guy who never lowered the toilet seat. He left the cap off of the toothpaste. Who's to say his forgetfulness wasn't a temporary blip?

Then quiet.

"Tim, Tim are you there?"

The silence sucked all the air out of the room. Finally, his brother spoke. Tim, a tennis pro in North Carolina, communicated with fill-in-the-blanks. "Am I supposed to…? You want me to…?"

No matter how he braced himself, Avery was never prepared for his brother's sleight of hand. A perpetual bachelor, Tim fulfilled all of his father's fantasies. While Avery sat in a law office and watched his muscles atrophy, Tim was tan with bulging biceps. Avery worked his ass off to buy his wife and children a house, two cars, a yard. Tim was three years younger and one paystub ahead of the bills.

If he applied himself he could have gone to college. But Tim got by on his good looks and easy charm. There was always a get-rich-quick scheme snapping in the wind. Over the years, he sweet-talked Murray into investing in more than one. His father never seemed to learn.

"You're giving him how much dough?" Avery would yell.

He couldn't remember an occasion where he leaned on his father. For money or advice. Hell, he couldn't remember his father ever giving him a hug. But Tim was different. He was always getting bailed out of trouble.

To Avery's disbelief, people found his neediness endearing. "He's a screw-up, Dad. He always screws up."

Murray would write him a check just the same. And usually fork it over with a slap on the back and an ear-to-ear grin.

Now his father had lost his mind and most of his money. When Arlene presented him with the divorce papers, he just signed on the dotted line. She got their home, half his savings, antiques that had been in the family for years. Murray moved into a one room rental with a pullout couch. A lifetime's worth of memories was stuffed into a filing cabinet the color of dirt.

"Where's Arlene?" asked Murray. "Where did Arlene go?"

The first week he circled the apartment like a hamster on a wheel. Avery had to stick Post-its on the walls and cabinet doors. Little yellow papers cried *Socks! Forks! Toilet paper!* He hid the knives and unplugged the stove. "Just use the microwave, Dad, okay?" His father looked at him like he was talking in Chinese. "Push this button, just one button, Dad."

Things went downhill so quickly Murray didn't know what hit him. The New York Times crossword would sit on the coffee table for days, blank and abandoned. Books were left with pristine spines. Charlotte, the kind of gal who left out bowls of milk for the neighborhood cats, brought groceries—his favorite cookies, cough drops, cereal. She'd make him a cup of green tea and write in big blocks letters on his calendar *Charlotte was here.*

"He's wiping his nose with a sock!" Avery told his brother on the phone. "He's peeing in his pants."

Little by little, Murray was stripped of his independence. It was like watching water heading down the drain. Circle, circle, gone.

First to go was the bicycle. One Tuesday Murray tried to ride around his new complex, fell down and couldn't get up. For hours he sat on the grass, smoothing the blades, humming the Andrews Sisters. He forgot his ID and had no idea how to use his cell phone.

When a good Samaritan called the cops, they hauled him into the management office. Luckily, the Super recognized him. "That's Murray. He's the new guy in 409." The Super was used to stray dogs and stray children but not this kind of headache. "I have his son's number. I have to call his son."

It was hard for Avery to take away the car keys. Murray liked to drive. And somehow the part of his brain that worked the car had stayed intact. He had a savantlike grasp of the neighborhood, instinctively grasping how to turn right and turn left. It was the where and when he couldn't figure out.

Wife number two heard about the divorce and revisited her prospects. Astrid was a masseuse from Denmark. Tall, blond, a midlife crisis cliché. Murray had dumped the mother of his children, his wife of twenty years, and tried to become a hippie. They bought a waterbed, lava lamp, grew their own vegetables. For a few years it worked. But Murray was too conventional, too Brooks Brothers, she told him. Her astrologer said their stars weren't aligned. She saw her future, and a Jewish stockbroker with a bulging paunch had no place in it.

But suddenly Astrid was older and wiser. She called Murray from Tampa. "I'd love to see you," she told him. "Why don't you come visit?" It took him three days to make the five-hour trip to the west coast, and another three days to get home.

Avery had been in a panic. "You went where? And exactly why?"

"She wants to get married. Astrid wants to marry me again." Murray smiled like a kid just offered a hot fudge sundae.

"Astrid's moving back to Miami?" asked Avery.

"No, No." said Murray with a goofy grin.

Avery fingered his wrist. His pulse was somersaulting. After a game of twenty questions, the pieces came together. It seemed that

Astrid's fluency in English had remarkably improved. Phrases like *financial security* and *long term planning* peppered her speech. She recalled exactly how much money was in Murray's retirement fund. And after he died, Murray's social security benefits wouldn't hurt either.

"Dad, I don't think there is a lot in this for you."

"We used to canoodle. I like to canoodle," Murray blurted.

"Does she want to live with you? Does she want to take care of you?"

"Astrid has a new friend. Otto or Anton, I forget." Then Murray's face went blank. Like someone had taken an eraser and wiped it clean. "Can you turn on the TV? I wanna watch TV."

When he was young, Avery dreaded playing catch with his father. He'd worried so much about dropping the ball that his hands would shake and his eyes would water. And sure enough he'd drop it. Suddenly he sensed that his father was slipping through his fingers. Bit by bit Murray's brain was shrinking like a dried sponge.

Avery needed to put his father's papers in order. He itched to search through Murray's filing cabinet but couldn't find the nerve. "It's like rummaging through his underwear," Avery told Charlotte. "He's entitled to his privacy. What else does he have left?"

Instead, he sat next to his father on the pullout couch and attempted a conversation. Each question was as wrenching and deliberate as a tooth extraction. "Do you have any insurance, Dad? Did you make out a will?"

Again, a goofy grin. "Call Max," his father answered. His longtime attorney, the same one who handled the divorce.

Max Weinstein had played golf with Murray for years. His voice was hoarse and unsteady, like someone who given up smoking twenty years too late. "Everything's going to the two of you. There's not much but everything's going to the two of you."

"I don't want his money," said Avery. "Give it to my kids instead." Charlotte's parents were always at their house. They taught Heather how to drive, clapped in the school auditorium whenever Sammy won awards. But Murray was just a furniture fixture. Someone who showed up on Thanksgiving and New Year's, filled his plate and stared at the flatscreen. Avery doubted he knew his kids' birthdays.

He sat down on the pullout with his father a second time. The papers from Weinstein's office rested in his lap. "Dad, I want you to sign here," he said. "This would give your grandchildren a little money."

Murray worked his jaw up and down like an elevator. "Okey dokey," he answered. Drool dripped down his chin. "You've got to accentuate the positive, eliminate the negative," he started singing. Then he picked his teeth with the pen.

Circle, circle, gone. Again he called his brother.

"We need to move him into an assisted living facility," Avery murmured into the phone. Tim had just finished remodeling his house, bought a convertible, taken a month long vacation to New Zealand. It seemed that one of his crazy investments actually paid off. Avery lobbed the big question. "Think you can chip in? It's going to be expensive."

On the other end of the line Tim let loose a long whistle. "Gee, Av. Everything's...tied up."

Avery sighed loudly—*This is a public service announcement* loud. "Dad's money's not gonna last long." He waited for a reply but the silence just expanded. Talking to his brother had always been like playing gin. You threw out a card and hoped for the best.Even with a winning hand, it always felt like losing.

Murray gradually lost the ability to dress himself, use the toilet, bathe. Every muscle memory was failing him. He'd stumble as he walked but forget to use the walker. He'd wolf down hamburgers but forget to chew. Within a year Murray needed to be moved to a nursing home. His confines had shriveled to a bed and a TV. Goodwill picked up the couch and Avery moved the filing cabinet into his garage. Murray's savings were all used up. He was a Medicaid patient now.

Every Sunday, Avery's family of four paid a visit. Thirteen-year-old Sammy, an Avery clone, would play the piano in the lounge while the old people nodded their heads, slapped their thighs. He was skinny with a mouth full of braces, the type of kid who kept statistics for the basketball team.

Heather, two years older, was suffering through her adolescence. Thick eyeliner made her look like a raccoon. Metal studs ran up and down her ears. She slumped on a folding chair, head down, texting her friends. Every few minutes she surfaced for air. "Grandpa never knew us," she sulked. "Do you really think he knows us now?"

When the hospice people were signed up, Tim finally made an appearance. It was like a movie star had entered their lives. Avery's children gushed. "Did you see his Facebook page?" Tim tweeted and Skyped while Avery was stuck in the medieval ages. "His playlist is awesome! Have you read his blog?"

But it had been over ten years since Tim had seen his father, and his star seemed to have lost its light. Murray's eyes lit up if Charlotte or Avery entered the room but Tim was invisible. His younger son sobbed at his bedside, shocked that he had become a stranger. "His mind's frozen in time," said Avery. "You don't look the way you used to. He doesn't realize who you are."

As soon as Murray had stopped eating, they knew it would only be a matter of days. Avery busied himself calling funeral homes and cemeteries. It was like buying a car. Economy packages threw in the memorial service if you bought the headstone and a plot. There was a special deal for buying early. "I hate to pressure you," said a salesman. "But if you commit before he dies there's a ten percent discount." Avery wrote down prices and researched coffins. Anything was easier than watching their father die.

After all the arrangements were made, when there were no other distractions Avery could cling to, he turned to his brother. They walked up and down the nursing home corridor like passengers on a cruise ship, nodding at every passerby, pinching their nostrils when the urine and disinfectant couldn't be ignored. Avery tried to talk about sports or the news but Tim always liked to dig deep.

"Ever wonder about Sammy?

Avery stopped short, his knees buckling. He looked around at the old guys in wheelchairs to make sure they weren't listening.

Tim plunged forward. "What I mean is..." Then a long pause. He turned up his hands and shrugged his shoulders. Another fill- in-the-blank. "You ever wonder what team he's playing for?"

Avery swallowed hard. "Sammy's not gay. He's an honor student, Tim. That's what they look like."

Another day Tim pummeled him with questions about Heather. Avery was terrified of his daughter. It was like an alien had landed in their home and taken over the body of their sweet little girl. She had a padlock on her bedroom door and a scowl that froze water. Tim forged ahead to fill the empty space. "You think Heather's a virgin?"

Avery glanced at the nurses' station.

"She's told you about the boyfriend, right?"

Avery had no idea Heather was dating. He wondered if his wife had a clue.

But Tim was just finding his rhythm. The words flew out. "And these days, they don't think blowjobs are sex. They go down on each other in the school bathrooms, in the cafeteria. It's like.... an extracurricular activity."

Avery felt his fingers stiffen. He wanted to kill his brother. Their mother was dead. Their father was dying. He wished he had been an only child.

That night he finally worked up the courage to open the drawers of his father's filing cabinet. He found a rag and wiped off the cobwebs. The smell of mildew made him gag. Dated tax returns were covered with furry black blotches. Old photographs curled.

Then he found a large envelope with the letters *IOUs* handwritten on the front. He opened it and tossed the contents on the kitchen table. Dozens of scrap papers cascaded out. Even cocktail napkins and matchbook covers. All of them were scribbled in Tim's writing with the date and amount. Avery envisioned his brother and his father sitting at a bar, his father opening his wallet, forking over bills, and Tim chicken-scratching numbers on whatever was handy. Avery took out a calculator and added up all the figures. There was over a hundred thousand dollars in IOUs splayed in front of him.

The next day he brought the envelope to the nursing home.

Murray had gotten worse overnight. "His breathing is rapid," said the nurse. "I can barely find his pulse." Charlotte sat by his bedside, held his hand and watched him struggle for each breath. His sons paced the halls.

"You owe Dad a lot of money," said Avery. "$101,200 to be exact." An aide was pushing a cart full of pills. She looked up, arched her eyebrows.

Tim planted his feet and stared at his brother. "Bullshit."

Avery waved the envelope in his face. "It's here. Every last IOU. It's right in here."

Brushing away the envelope, Tim slapped Avery's hand. "They were gifts. I don't have to pay back a cent. Dad loved me. I don't have to pay back a cent."

"It's in writing, Tim."

Avery edged closer but Tim held his ground. Practically growled through his teeth. "You can fucking sue me."

Avery felt the cords on his neck throb. The walls were closing in. "You're not gonna screw me again. This money belongs to my kids."

He cocked back his right fist and let it fly. Tim caught the punch on his cheekbone, spun. Then he turned around and head-butted his brother. The nurse's aide dodged just in time but they hit the cart. Hundreds of plastic bottles rolled on the linoleum. They were locked in an embrace, shoving and jabbing, hurtling themselves against the walls.

Charlotte ran into the hallway. "Avery! Tim!" she shouted.

Avery pushed his brother out of the way, stood up straight, and combed his fingers through his hair. His shirttail was out and blood was dripping from his arm. Bruises on Tim's face were blooming purple and red blotches. "We'll be quiet. We'll be good. Sorry. Sorry."

"It's just that..." Charlotte looked down. She wiped a tear from her eye. "Your father's dead. He just passed. "

Tim buried his head in his hands. "Oh God!" he cried. "How will I live without him?" Tears wracked his body. His cries shook the windows. Wisps of white hair peered from doorways to see what the tumult was about.

Avery collapsed on the floor, deflated. Now he would always be a ghost. His father's approval would be beyond his grasp, his brother's love as disembodied as a dream. On the wall he saw a shadow. Crouched, the figure of a man tucked into a ball. He touched it slowly to see if it was real.

About the author:

Marlene Olin was born in Brooklyn, raised in Miami, and educated at the University of Michigan. Her short stories have been published in *The Saturday Evening Post* online, *WIPS Journal*, *Vine Leaves*, *Biostories*, *Emrys Journal*, *Poetica*, *Arcadia*, and *The Jewish Literary Journal*. They are forthcoming in *Edge*, *Ragazine*, *The Podras Review*, and *Meat for Tea*. Two of her stories will be anthologized in collections next year. She has recently completed her first novel.

SEARCHING FOR ALEXANDRA CHAMPION
©2015 by Dana C. Smith

Ben crossed Fourth Avenue at a brisk pace, trying to beat the countdown of the blinking lights. He leapt to the curb to avoid stepping in a puddle. When he landed, he noticed a homeless woman hovering underneath the Macy's awning at the corner of Fourth and Pine. She was holding a cardboard sign he didn't read because he knew it would be like all the others: *Hungry. Please help. Will work for food. God bless.* She was a large-framed, haggard-looking creature dressed in layer upon layer of baggy clothing that hung on her like dirty bathrobes. What caught his eye was her shoes. They were tied in plastic bags, and not just one bag, but several bags on each foot. Ben averted his eyes and tilted his umbrella to hide the woman from his view. He quickened his pace and forged ahead with determination, but no clear destination. He was no more than ten feet away from the woman when he spotted a blue, wallet-sized notebook face-down on the sidewalk. It looked like a flimsy address book. He didn't make a practice of picking up street trash, but there was something particularly alluring about this object. He turned the book right side up and discovered it was something far more valuable than an address book. It was a passport—a Canadian passport.

He paused for a moment, somewhat surprised the homeless

woman hadn't bothered to claim the passport as her own. There was an official-looking Canadian government seal stamped in gold on the outside cover. The back pages were filled with fine print written in English and French. There was no money tucked away between the soggy pages, no interesting stamps, nothing at all but her beautiful face, a string of names and her signature. Alexandra Marie Champion.

Ben looked around for a possible owner, but the sidewalks were thinly populated that rainy Sunday morning. He dropped the passport in his messenger bag, feeling somewhat relieved Alexandra Champion was not in the area. That gave him more time to spend with her—not the real Alexandra but the woman in the picture, the one he was inexplicably drawn to.

He settled into an overstuffed chair at Starbucks. Between sips of coffee he examined every detail of the passport. She was born in White Rock, British Columbia, on September 10, 1990. Twenty-three years old. The perfect age. There was no address, phone number, not even an emergency contact. He inspected the numbers, letters, and dashes shaped like less-than signs trailing the glossy border of the identification page. It was her picture he focused on the longest. She had a swan-like neck, oval-shaped face and eyebrows arched to widen the appearance of her doe eyes. Her rose-colored lips were fixed in a curious expression. Her hair appeared to be in a French braid, or at least braided from a side part, then pulled away from her face. Ben imagined her to have the delicate body of a ballerina and the long legs of a runway model.

He put his coffee cup on a side table and gazed out the window. The rain drizzling down the panes of glass, combined with the hissing sound from the cappuccino maker, created a hypnotizing ambience. What was she doing in Seattle on a Saturday night? It must have been Saturday. Certainly somebody would have picked up the passport if it was there longer than a day. He imagined Alexandra walking down Pine Street with her girlfriends, laughing, stumbling a bit in her high heels, then laughing some more when she bumped into one of her friends, causing both girls to lose their balance. They might have been headed to one of the bars near Pike Place Market. It was raining. Yes, it had to be raining. She was in a hurry. He could see them, Alexandra and her friends, sharing an umbrella. Alexandra adjusted the strap of her purse higher on her shoulder and tightened her coat around her waist. The jerking motion was swift enough to send the contents of her bag skittering across the sidewalk. Ben imagined himself rushing to her side to help collect her things. Their eyes would meet. She would feel the intense chemical attraction too. It's the way lovers meet—suddenly, unexpectedly.

Ben felt the vibration of the phone in his coat pocket. Susan's name flashed on the screen.

"When are you coming home?" she said abruptly.

He could feel his heart rate begin to rise, the way it did when he stopped short in traffic. He stroked the back of his wedding band with his thumb and said, "Tomorrow night. I told you. Couldn't get a flight out until after five."

"Take a cab. I'm not picking you up."

"I don't expect you to."

Susan began shouting a litany of insults at him, the same complaints he'd heard so many times he couldn't listen to them anymore. You're never home. I have to do everything. The kids don't know you. I'm sick of this. I want out.

He held the phone a few inches away from his ear, but the distance did nothing to lessen the prickly tone of Susan's voice. He glanced at the seat across from his. There was Alexandra with her arms casually draped across the back of the chair, long legs crossed, and her skirt pushed up to her mid-thigh.

"You're married," she said. Her voice was sultry and there was a hint of a French accent.

"Yes," he whispered.

"Then what are you doing here with me?"

Ben heard the pump and grinding of a city bus as it pulled away from the stop outside the coffee shop. He glanced out the window for a second. When he turned back to Alexandra, she was gone.

"Did you hear me?" Susan shouted.

"Maybe I'll wait until Tuesday morning, Tuesday night at the latest," he said, then hung up the phone even though Susan was still talking.

Things weren't always like this with Susan. She liked spending time with him. She used to laugh at his jokes and hang on every word. "You're so clever, Benji," she'd say to him. She never said *smart* or *funny*—just *clever*. It was Susan who usually initiated sex and Ben considered himself lucky to have a wife who was so adventurous. But something changed in their seventh year of marriage. The *seven year itch*, his friends called it. But Ben never worried about what other people considered a pivotal point in a marriage. He and Susan were together seven years before they got married. He knew her better than anyone, or so he thought. She used to like to travel. Now she rarely left home. Her moods were as temperamental as the weather, more so since the girls were born. She wanted a husband who worked nine to five and would always be home for dinner, not a man whose job required him to travel the globe. The more he traveled, the more she seemed to resent him. But she liked the money. Always happy to spend his money. Being a wife to him—a real wife, the wife he deserved—was too much for her.

When he suggested she see a therapist or ask her doctor for an antidepressant, she would get angry and lash out, "You'd love that, wouldn't you, Benji? Get your *crazy* wife on some *crazy* pills just to shut her up. If I'm crazy, it's your fault. You're the one driving me insane!" Then she'd lock herself in the bedroom for hours, crying while the girls whined outside the door, "Mommy, why are you crying?"

Susan would say, "Daddy makes me cry!" Then all three of them would start crying. It was too much. He deserved better, so much better than all the tears and bitching and fighting, only to have her beg him not to leave her once she calmed down.

On his way back to the hotel, he paid special attention to every woman he passed on the street. He retraced his steps back to Fourth and Pine. Even the homeless woman had disappeared. He began to question if she was ever there at all. Maybe it was divine intervention.

Had he not turned away to avoid making eye contact with her, he might not have seen the passport.

He was a block away from the hotel when he spotted a tall slender woman ahead of him. She had long, wavy light brown hair that flowed down the middle of her back. She carried herself with the grace and confidence of a woman of good breeding. He picked up his pace. "Hey," he called to her. He waved the passport. "Did you drop this?"

The woman stopped and turned to him. She was older, perhaps late forties. She had a sharp chin, up-turned nose, thin lips, and a ruddy complexion. She shook her head, turned and walked away without saying a word. Back at the hotel, he stood at the elevator, pressing the UP button at a staccato rate. The doors opened. There was a woman inside with her head lowered. She was fishing around in her purse as if she was searching for lost keys.

"Alexandra?" he said.

She looked up. Young enough, he thought, but it wasn't her. Not his Alexandra.

"Sorry, I thought you were someone else."

He couldn't get back to his room fast enough. He shed his coat, reached inside his bag and pulled out his laptop. How would she be able to return to Canada without her passport? He had to save her. He opened his laptop and was briefly distracted by the screensaver of his daughters Maggie, age five, with her gap-tooth smile, and Grace, two years younger, blowing kisses. They looked exactly like Susan; both of them little carbon copies of their mother. He would deny their paternity if it wasn't for their eyes—blue as the sky on a clear day. When people used to rave over the girls' beautiful eyes, Susan would say, "Just like Ben's." Now she claimed their eye color as a recessive trait on her side of the family. It was like Ben didn't exist, like he had no part in bringing the children into the world. He was in the delivery room when they were born. He was the first person to hold them. Now the distance between he and the girls was almost as wide as the gulf that separated he and Susan. He preferred not to think about it, chalking their closeness to their mother up to their ages, and being girls. If he had a son, maybe things would be different.

Ben lightly tapped the keyboard and the picture of his daughters vanished. He typed Alexandra's name in the search engine. Up popped a *LinkedIn* Alexandra Champion, and several Facebook profile connections. The *LinkedIn* Alexandra lived in London, had copper-colored hair and worked in public relationships for an investment firm. He entered *Alexandra Marie Champion* in the search field of his Facebook account. There were only two profiles of twenty-something women in Canada with the same face shape, brown hair and symmetrical features similar to the Alexandra in the passport. He clicked on a profile for Alexandra Champion from Vancouver. There were two other girls in her profile picture. He tried to hone in on which one of the girls matched the passport photo, but the person most prevalently pictured had a fuller face and higher brow line. Her hair was dull and flat. She was heavy-set with a tattoo of a lotus blossom on her shoulder that extended toward her right breast.

There was an Alexandra Champion from Ontario. She had a lip ring. Her eyes were heavily lined in black. He noticed a streak of purple hair on one side of her face. His Alexandra had the pure features of an angel. She would never wear a smoky-eye, or pierce and tattoo her body.

He continued to search variations of her name, perhaps Marie Champion, Alex, or Ali. There was nothing wrong with looking at personal pictures of women he didn't know. He was only doing what any Good Samaritan would do. He sent messages to two women on Facebook who looked vaguely familiar. *Did you lose a passport in downtown Seattle? What is your address? I'll send it to you.*

When Ben felt like he'd exhausted all leads, he entered the words *found Canadian passport* in Google. The Canadian Consulate was on the same street as his hotel and only a block away from where he found the passport. It was all too much of a coincidence—the hotel, the Canadian Consulate, the passport, the girl. Maybe he didn't find the passport. The passport found him. Some cosmic force brought this woman into his life. Searching for Alexandra Champion was no longer an option. It was an obligation.

That night, Ben rolled over in bed and felt the warm presence of a woman's body. Her hair smelled like jasmine. He kissed her on the back of her neck and ran his fingers along the smooth contours of her body. Her skin was soft and her breasts firm, the way Susan's were early in their marriage when things were good. He wrapped his arms around her and pulled her close. Their bodies fit together perfectly, like pieces of a puzzle. For the first time in years, Ben was able to relax. Being with Alexandra felt uncomplicated, simple and so right it was easy for him to forget what was waiting for him at home. When he woke up, he found himself hugging a pillow. His legs were entwined in sheets and a comforter, not Alexandra's body. He closed his eyes and prayed. *Back to the dream, dear God. Please. Back to the dream.*

Monday morning, he walked around downtown Seattle within the boundaries of the city blocks from the hotel to the Canadian Consulate, and back to the street corner where he found the passport. He took a seat outside Westlake Center where he watched and waited for the building that housed the Canadian Consulate to open. He sipped a vanilla latte and searched every face in the hustle and bustle crowd. Maybe she was waiting for the office to open, too. An hour passed before Ben exhausted his people watching. He knew what he had to do. It was the right thing, the only thing that made sense.

He entered the sixth floor suite of the Consulate, hoping Alexandra would be there waiting for him, but there was nobody in the vast office space except a young man sitting behind a bank teller-type glass booth.

"I found a passport," Ben said. "Is this where I turn it in?"

"Yes. Thank you," the man replied.

"Has anyone reported one missing?"

"Not that I'm aware."

Ben fingered the passport in his coat pocket. He hesitated a bit before he said, "I don't have it with me. Just wanted to make sure this is the right place. I'll bring it by later."

Ben exited the building feeling somewhat lighter and happier than he'd felt since he landed in Seattle. He'd keep it, just for a while. He could mail it back to the Consulate when he got home. No harm in hanging on to it a few more days. There was still a chance he'd find Alexandra. It would be so much better for him to hand the passport over to her in person. No reward necessary, he'd tell her. He'd offer to buy her a cup of coffee, or better yet, ask her to join him for dinner.

* * *

The first day of spring marked a ritual Susan Elliott had performed since she graduated from college. It was the day she stored her winter gear and moved her spring and summer wardrobe forward in the closet rotation. Over the years the task grew in size to include her husband's suits, and, later, the nice coats and dresses her parents had given the girls to wear to church. Even though she'd taken to stepping over Ben's dirty dress shirts scattered on the floor of their walk-in closet, just to see how long it would take him to tend to his own dry cleaning, she chose to be the better person and add the Brooks Brothers garments he liked heavily starched to the pile. She went to the coat closet to retrieve her wool coat, then back to the bedroom to add a few of her nicer sweaters to the collection. When she got in the car, she put the key in the ignition but remembered there was something she missed. She went back in the house to get Ben's coat. She checked the pockets as she always did on laundry days. It was not unusual for Ben to leave loose change, keys, breath mints or his wallet in his coat and pants pockets. She felt something stiff tucked away in the inside coat pocket, like a wallet, but not as thick. It was a passport. Canada. A woman, Alexandra Marie Champion. She lowered her head and began to cry. *Not this again.*

She took the passport and hid it in the junk drawer in the kitchen. She'd confront him later. She had to pull herself together first, get a plan, figure out how she'd explain things to the girls. He couldn't see her cry. This time she'd be strong. She thought about the hang up calls from unknown numbers and the cryptic text messages Ben was always able to explain away. There were the business trips that lasted a few days longer than planned. He changed the passwords to his phone and e-mail accounts every time Susan figured out the codes.

It wasn't until after they were married that she discovered there was a side of her husband she didn't know, and might never know because he was so good at keeping secrets. "You're paranoid," he'd say to her. "You're imaging things." But there was no denying the pictures the private investigator took of Ben in a bar in San Antonio with another woman on his lap, or the phone numbers to female voices she'd discovered in his pockets over the years. Gather evidence. That's what her attorney told her. If she wanted full custody, there had to be more evidence.

Weeks later, she was watching a *Dateline* episode and heard a name she recognized.

> *"The news that family and friends of Alexandra Champion feared most was confirmed last Friday when the body of the 23-year-old Canadian woman was recovered off the coast of Puget Sound. Champion, an art student, was reported missing Monday, February 24th when she failed to show up for her job as a docent at the Seattle Art Museum. She was last seen Friday, February 21st exiting the Whiskey Bar on Second Avenue in downtown Seattle with an unidentified man in his late thirties wearing a black coat and blue jeans. Please call the Seattle Police Department or Crime Stoppers at 1-800-891-HELP for suspect tips or leads."*

Susan calmly reached for the phone and dialed the number. "I have information about the missing woman—the Champion girl," she said to the detective.

About the author:

Dana C. Smith is the author of the non-fiction stories *Season of Melancholy* and *I'll Love You Forever, or Until the Cameras Stop Rolling* published in the on-line magazine division of *Ladies Home Journal*. She is also the 2007 winner of the non-fiction category for the annual summer writing competition sponsored by the Vanderbilt University Medical Center magazine *House Organ*. She has studied at the Writer's Loft at Middle Tennessee State University and began her MFA studies in 2013 at the University of Arkansas at Monticello. Dana was recently awarded a scholarship to Spalding University to complete her MFA degree. Dana currently works as a hospital pharmacist at Vanderbilt Children's Hospital in Nashville, Tennessee.

TWINKLE
©2015 by Paul Andrews

The old man's skin was so weathered you could have made shoes out of it. He sat there next to me on the picnic table, as still as a cigar store Indian, just staring up at the early evening sky. It was a cloudless day and, this far from city smog; the sky actually looked blue instead of brown. The sun kissed the western horizon, offering a spectacular vista, but the man stared almost directly overhead. As to what fixed his attention so firmly I could not tell. Not a bird flew overhead, not even an airplane. All my questions had returned nothing but a series of 'Yeps' and 'Nopes.' I was at a loss as to what to do next.

I first saw the old gent this afternoon as I was driving out of the city on an errand. He was just walking on the side of the road by himself, a lone figure amongst the zipping traffic. The snow white hair and slow pace caught my eye.

Better walking than driving, I thought, nothing worse than some old-timer behind the wheel of a big old land yacht doing 35 in 55 mph zone. But, something made me stop. I don't know why. Living in the city it's ingrained in you to ignore everyone: people you pass on sidewalks, the homeless begging on corners, those sitting across from you on the subway. Nevertheless, I pulled over and waited for him to catch up. I lowered the window on my SUV.

"You all right, old man?" I asked, shouting out the window. I immediately chastised myself for being rude. My parents would've given me a good lecture about respecting your elders. I should have called him *mister* or *sir*.

"Yep," he said, without stopping. "Just fine. Thanks for asking."

The man was dressed in a pair of faded blue jeans, red flannel shirt, and nylon jacket. A new baseball cap sat on his head and a decent pair of sneakers covered his feet. He carried a small plastic shopping bag. He didn't look like a vagrant, nor someone suffering from dementia. His eyes looked sharp and clear.

"Where you headed?" I asked next, keeping pace with my accelerator.

"Oh, just up the road a bit," he responded.

Just up the road could mean anything from the next intersection to Canada.

"Need a lift?" Again, I couldn't believe I was asking this. You never, ever picked up a hitcher nowadays. They could be drug addicts, terrorists, or even serial killers.

Here, the man finally stopped walking and stared at me a second. "Yeah, I sure could."

And that was that. He climbed into my SUV with little difficulty. His tanned, world-weary face looked to be at least eighty, but given his pace, he could have been younger. He barely said a word while we drove. I tried small talk but it got me nowhere.

"You live around here?"

"Yep."

"Going to visit someone?"

"Nope."

He seemed more interested in the sky than anything I had to say. He constantly looked up out the windshield.

We left the suburbs behind and started to enter a more rural section. Nothing but forest, farms or horse ranches lined the road. Suddenly, out of the blue, he asked to be let out.

"This ought to do," he said simply.

"You mean right here?" I asked.

"Yep."

"I can't take you any farther?"

"Nope."

I shrugged and pulled over. There was nothing in sight but a line of tall pines trees on the right and a deep pasture on the left.

"You sure about this?" I asked.

"Yep." The old man got out and slammed the door shut. "Much obliged."

This is where my city 'tude finally kicked in. Fine, I thought, if the old fool wants to kill himself by walking off into the wilderness then so be it. I'd probably read about him in the newspaper in a few days:

ELDERLY MAN FOUND DEAD ALONGSIDE ROUTE 98

I had better things to do, places to get to. "Suit yourself," I said and drove on. Part of me felt bad, but I would forget about the old man soon enough. I had a busy day ahead of me. I felt sure that was the last I'd ever see of him.

That is, until later that afternoon.

I finished my business in the next town and headed back to the city. I had the windows down and my satellite radio blasting. Life was good. That was when I saw him again. He was sitting on the side of the road this time, on one of those lone picnic tables at a roadside pull off.

I drove on by him at first. The crazy old fool, I thought. I did not need to get involved again. I had big plans for tonight and did not need to waste time on some stranger. But, instead, I found my foot slamming on the brake as I steered into the gravel shoulder.

I got out and walked back to him. He was just sitting there on the picnic bench, staring up at the evening sky, just like he'd been doing in my SUV. He was facing a pasture that stretched out to a tree-lined horizon. Not much traffic filled the road, with only the occasional car passing by.

"Hey," I said, "we meet again."

The old man glanced down just a second and I saw him sigh, as if saying 'Oh, you again.' Then he returned his gaze to the sky. "Yep."

I looked up at the darkening sky overhead. It was an ocean of unbroken blue in all directions. The sun was setting near the western horizon but the man stared off to the south. I, of course, could not see a damn thing, not a hawk, not even a jet trail.

"Pretty day," I started.

"Yep."

"Uh, just what are you doing way out here?"

The man broke his upward gaze for just a second and met my eyes. "Thanks for stopping, but I'm just fine."

"That's all right. I needed a break." I was not going anywhere without an answer. "So, what are you doing out here?"

He returned his gaze to the sky and seemed resigned to the fact I was not leaving. "Waitin'."

"OK. What exactly are you waiting *for*?" I looked at the sky again. "And what are you looking at?"

His eyes were slightly squinted, forming a fan of deep crows feet on either side. They were a clear ice blue, no sign of cloudiness or cataracts. "Nothing, at the moment."

"You expecting something?" I asked, but immediately cursed myself for asking another yes/no question.

The old man's answer did not disappoint. "Yep."

It was like talking to a teenager. "What are you waiting for?"

The man sighed again and I could tell I was getting on his nerves. Good, maybe I'd get more than monosyllable answers out of him.

"Just a sign," he answered finally.

A sign? What the hell did that mean? A skydiver, a blimp, angels from heaven, a freaking UFO? I liked sci-fi as much as the next guy but wouldn't hike to the middle of nowhere to stare at the sky all day long. Doing it at his age raised all sorts of red flags, mainly dementia. Maybe he wandered away from his family and they were looking for him right now.

The sky was starting to darken and I suddenly had a thought. "You mean like in space?"

"Yep," he answered.

"The stars?" They'd certainly be coming out soon.

"Nope."

All right, now I had to do something. The old kook must have wandered away from a retirement home expecting aliens to come get him. But what should I do now? *Don't get involved,* my instincts warned me. I could just get in my SUV and leave him behind. He might die of exposure overnight, though. I could call 911, but tell them what? The police would ask a bunch of questions, making me late for a big night. I had what I hoped would be a hot date with a girl from my apartment complex.

I sighed and sat down next to him. I decided to give it one more chance before bailing. "You been here all afternoon?"

"Yep."

"Aren't you thirsty or hungry or something?"

The man pointed to a crumpled grocery bag and bottle of water near his feet. "Brought supper."

For the first time I noticed a compass sitting in the palm of his right hand and an old pocket watch in the other. They looked worn and well-tarnished.

"Well, how long are you going to stay out here?"

He took a quick glance down at his pocket watch. "A bit more."

"It gets pretty cold at night, you know."

"Night's too late. It'll happen before then."

"Some kind of sign then?" I asked.

The old man checked the compass in his other hand and turned back to the sky. "Yep."

"I don't suppose, you'd want to come back with me now would you?"

"Nope."

"Yeah, didn't think so."

And that's what brought me to this point. I was at a loss as to what to do next. I figured the best thing was to call 911. Tell them this crazy old coot was sitting out here waiting for a sign from outer space. I shouldn't do it where he could see me, though. "Well, I'm going to go now."

"Suit yourself, much obliged for the ride."

I stood up to leave. Just then the old man gasped in a breath. He squinted his eyes at the sky and broke out into the biggest, broadest smile I'd ever seen on a person that old. He laughed out loud and slapped his knee. "I'll be damned. I'll be God damned, there it is"

I immediately looked up at the darkening sky and saw nothing. "There what is?"

He raised an arm into the air and pointed. I saw nothing at first, but then, in the southern sky about 30 degrees up from the horizon, something twinkled, then vanished. The sun had just dropped below the western horizon. I squinted my own eyes and I saw it again. Something definitely twinkled and then vanished. It wasn't a star, the sky was still too bright for any. It was like the sun reflecting off a...off a spaceship!

My God, something *was* up there. It was too far away to be a jet or a plane. It had to be something in space. After about the sixth twinkle it stopped.

The old man sighed next to me and I turned to look at him. It was as if I was staring at a different person. The expressionless face from earlier had vanished. His whole face was alive with joy and something else; it took me a while to second to realize it: contentment. I noticed a tear rolling down his leathery cheek. He started talking to me then, freely and openly, as if I was an old acquaintance.

"You know, when ya get old, they tell you not to live your life through your children. You're supposed to let them leave the nest and live their own lives. But I don't agree." He touched a hand to his chest. "Ya see, we leave a tiny piece of our soul in each one them. So that part of us continues, even after we're nothing but dust in the dirt."

He turned back to the navy blue sky overhead. "I was a pilot when I was your age. Flew for the Army Air Corps in World War II." He stopped here and sighed deeply. "God, how I loved to fly. Everybody should have one thing in their lives they feel they were born to do and for me it was that. I couldn't be in the air enough. Couldn't go high enough, couldn't fly long enough. I'd take my plane up till the air was so thin I could barely breathe and the frost would coat the windows." He stretched an arm overhead. "The sky would be so dark above me, I'd reach up and could almost touch outer space. 'Course, back then you couldn't go any higher; but oh how I wished I could. How I wished I could fly right into space."

"That sounds real cool." I had a bland bank job that never reached that level of excitement, and probably never would. I often wondered what it would be like to have a more passionate profession. One I'd wake up anxious to get to every morning. But this man had lived it. He was one of a dying breed. America's Greatest Generation who had fought Hitler and won.

"My son caught the flying bug early on and was a test pilot during Vietnam. He applied for the astronaut program but was turned down. Only the luckiest people in the world ever get into space. Would've made me the proudest dad on earth, though." He looked at stars just starting to appear overhead. "But ya know, if you wait long enough, sometimes your dreams finally catch up with you."

"What do you mean? What exactly *was* that?"

He pointed a finger to where the twinkles were. "That's my granddaughter up there, on the International Space Station. She told me she'd give me a sign today as they passed over the US. She'd tilt the solar panels of the station and try to catch the sun just right, just enough to send a signal down to earth, down to her old Grandpop." He choked up for a moment and had to pause. "In my honor, she said, as the first of the family leave the ground behind."

I noticed tears filling the old man's eyes and he began to sniffle.

"She finally made it to space, but I was the first to fly. Now my great-grandson is flying model airplanes." He blew his nose into a red handkerchief.

Suddenly it all made sense: the long hike, the pocket watch, the compass. I was surprised to find tears welling up in my own eyes. "And she told you the best place to see it, didn't she? When and where to look."

"Yep, I had to get away from the city lights and the smog to get the best view."

"Wow," I mumbled, but it was nowhere adequate to describe this man's amazing moment. I chastised myself for categorizing the old gent as the discardable elderly. How jaded and wrong I was.

One question remained. "But, why walk?"

"They won't let me drive no more." He turned to me and grinned, a twinkle coming to his own eyes. "But I wasn't going to let that stop me."

"Why didn't you have someone else drive?"

"Well, my wife passed away years ago and the kids all live in other states. The retirement home I live in couldn't spare anyone to take me."

I smiled at his determination. I hoped to have a fraction of it when I reached his age, not to mention the legacy of such devoted grandchildren. I could barely hold on to a girlfriend for more than a month, let alone imagine such a thing.

"How did you plan to get back?"

The man pulled a cell phone out of his jacket pocket. "Figured I'd call the retirement home about now." He smiled mischievously. "Imagine they've noticed I'm gone."

I broke into a laugh. "Yep, I imagine they have. Well, sir, can I offer you a drive back?"

The gentleman turned to me and nodded. "I'd be much obliged." He reached up one last time and closed his fingers around where the twinkles had been. "We may not be able to live our lives completely through our children." He brought his closed hand down to his chest. "But right now, a part of me is right up there, and that's good enough for me."

About the author:

Paul Andrews was born and raised in the mountains of rural Pennsylvania. He has been writing short stories, novels and novellas for over twenty years. While his heart lies with historical mysteries & thrillers, he has also dabbled in science fiction, romance and even the paranormal. The Man Who Would Not Die is his first epublished novel, but he has many other stories to tell. Paul has a BS from Penn State, a graduate degree from Rutgers University and spent many successful years as a R&D project manager. After working for a time in Manhattan and Washington D.C, he slowly migrated south to warmer climes. He now works, lives and writes in North Carolina with his wife, their two children, and two cats.

www.ingramcontent.com/pod-product-compliance
Lightning Source LLC
Chambersburg PA
CBHW071307130626
46556CB00004B/1501